To Cindy

Corin Kim
4/27/16

Tears of the Yangtze

Published by:

Coreeilbo.com
9108 Church St. #306
Manassas, VA 20108
http://www.coreeilbo.com

Printed by:

Hanaindigo.
Nam-Dong 142 Bun-Ji, Dong-Gu, Kwangju, South Korea.

Cover Design and Layout: Audytama Studio

ISBN-10: 0-9975036-0-2
ISBN-13: 978-0-9975036-0-9

Thanks to,

I dedicate my heart to my husband John, who stood by me with encouragement and companionship through this journey with tremendous help from my daughter Dara and my generous son Arthur.

Table of Contents

Disclaimer

"The world as we have created it is a process of our thinking. It cannot be changed without changing our thinking."

—Albert Einstein —

One

It wasn't until two years after moving to Riverside, that she found out about the monthly poetry reading held by the various community members. She happened to come across a sign attached on the front door, "Poetry Reading Night." It was to be held at "Mundo," a café located on the intersection of Taylor Road and Pork Rock Parkway between seven and nine PM every third Thursdays. The advertisement was attached to another advertisement looking for "Tennis members," and these all had perforated edges the size of a thumb with phone numbers on them; there were gaps where someone had taken them, and the remaining pieces fluttered in the wind.

And about three years on a random Thursday, Hannah attended her first poetry night.

When she opened the doors of Café Mundo, she found a group of ten or so people sitting in a group. They were drinking tea and reading their and each other's poems. With Rachmaninov's Piano Concerto No. 2 Minor in the background, the whole scene looked cosy yet romantic. This atmosphere made Hannah's unfamiliar visit gentler; the mood drew her in. As Hannah had always been a bit introverted, she sat down in the far back corner, where it was slightly dimmer. Since it was her first time, she went empty-handed, and empty-hearted. Next to her was a young woman. She had a clean and glowing face free of make up, and was slender with a long neck. Her vivid features and bright eyes made Hannah think that this woman held a special occupation. She sat quietly, with her back straight. As most of the population living in Riverside were aged somewhere in their sixties, it made Hannah think that this woman didn't quite belong in this town. There were a few teenagers living with their grandparents due to the stableness and the quietness of the town, although during summer, more teenagers would hang out by the river, loudly running the boat motor and laughing.

After a simple introduction, Poetry Night began, and as everyone carefully listened and held their breath, the night continued to ripen, their voices filling the small space.

The woman sitting next to Hannah introduced herself as Summer Wu and held out her hand for Hannah to shake. She was a Chinese-American living across the river, but she stated that she came over to the Riverside community on Thursdays as a form of excursion. Hannah introduced herself as Hannah Walter. Since meeting each other, Hannah and Summer had become fast-stead friends for the past three years, growing their friendship through their attendance at the Poetry Night.

Most of the poetry sang the beauty of nature and the lives by the river. Summer's poems however, were different and special. She made people ponder about something else. For example, one of her poems expressed the loss and recovery of philanthropism associated with historical events. The light scent of Camilla poured over from the tea cup and sat lightly on Hannah's table. As they all sat next to each other, the scent of tea wrapped around us, taking away the stress of daily life and unwinding the knot holding their spirit tight. The light background music of the tea shop was open to poetry on that relaxed and sparsely populated shopping center of Thursday evening.

The most frequent patrons included Sandy, Kelly, Amy, Mr. Land, Mr. Anderson, Mr. Nelson and his wife, Mr. Harrison and his wife Jane. Except for the Summer, the rest lived in Riverside. Yet everytime they met, Hannah couldn't help but feel that Summer was a resident of Riverside commonfolk, rather than as a resident of the richer neighborhood across the river. Her make-up free face, relaxed attire, and honest smile made it difficult for Hannah to imagine Summer as the pretentious rich leading their fancy and outlandish lifestyle across the river. Summer was an unmarried woman in her mid to late thirties, yet looked to be a college student, giving off the mood of a rose filled with dew. She had curves in the right place, and her glow seemed obvious thanks to a regimented exercise and muscles.

Compared to her, Hannah was starting to see tiny freckles on her face; from the outside, her long hair made her look thirty, yet her joints didn't move as quite as fast as they used to, and the occasionally sprouting white-gray hair would spark under the light and make their existence known; she would be thoroughly annoyed by them. Yet for the most part, in all appearance to an outsider, she was a gorgeous woman in her early 30's. She hadn't had any work done nor gotten a botox, but chose to dye her hair a light brown color. When she let her hair down to go out, a few men would glance in her direction as they drove off, as age hadn't affected her much at all.

As they met once a month, the members got to know each other better; but Summer and Hannah met at least three or four times a month. Sometimes, Summer would appear at the shops Hannah visited, and as they shopped, they would exchange conversations and stories, eventually becoming close friends.

During Poetry Nights, Mundo's owner Alice would make special items to be consumed by the members, or old lady Jane's delicious casserole dishes would cause them to become more talkative. Old lady Jane's warm smiles made Hannah feel special. Jane always brought a plate to their events, and the members always praised her skills and loved her. Mrs. Nelson would make small snacks and make Mr. Nelson carry them to the event as well. Hannah began to bring various baked items as well. Every six months, the group selected their poems and sent it to be published by the local Riverside Community newspaper. It usually made headlines in the small town with no other exciting news. Last year, Hannah's poem was published on the community culture section.

After her poem was published, people outside of the poetry circle began to recognize her. Mr. Ford next door must have read the community newspaper, as he recognized her and was nicer to her. Clint even took the paper into work to boast about it at work.

Two

Clint must have had already left for work today as well, as the place next to her was cold and empty. These days, he basically lived at work. Hannah never knew when her husband returned home, but she'd feel around the bed for warmth to know it was him. As Hannah walked towards the kitchen, she found a mug with leftover coffee and the red light of the coffee maker still on. She poured herself a cup, and sat down on the table to find bagel crumbs and a tub of closed strawberry cream cheese Clint must have used on the bagel. Clint had taken his cup of coffee and bagel to start the early day once more, leaving an empty house yet again.

After Hannah finished her cup of coffee, she poured herself another cup, placed three chocolate chip cookies on a plate, and walked to her room. The morning light flowed into the room through the linen curtains, creating calming waves. The sunlight shined on the messy bed and the unfinished poem she worked on last night. As Hannah opened the window, the morning breeze brought in the slightly fishy smells of the river. Hannah took the futon off of the bed out to the deck to air it out, and couldn't help but think of the frozen land Amure's ladies. As the ladies of the Amure shook out the carpet after a long winter, Hannah also shook and tapped at the bedding airing it out completely. As she stood there staring outside while the bedding hung on the rail, she decided that his smell would ride the sunlight and fly away like a butterfly. There was a time in Hannah's life when she had paid complete attention to her husband, Clint. Decades ago, Clint was especially popular among the ladies at work, and that would irk Hannah's jealousy to no end. However, after she began to raise her children, she began to realize the utter uselessness of feeling this way. As her life began to revolve around her children, all of those memories held less weight, as Hannah began to think, "Oh, so it happened again," or "Oh, I guess she likes him a bit."

Hannah had square jaw like her father, and this difference made her the butt of jokes among her siblings. Because only one of her eyes had the double eyelid fold, her eye sizes would look different unless the onlooker was close by, which gave her siblings another reason to make fun of her. However, as she grew older, the eyelid drooped, and eyes no longer looked different. Her tall and straight nose was always the symbol of her older sister's envy. As she had participated in every exercise and sport as a child, she was thin and toned with a clear skin, and never wore make-up. She thought back to her past, as she cleaned the bathroom and looked at her reflection in the bathroom mirror.

After marrying Clint, she continued to age beautifully. As Hannah began to dye her hair light brown, she aged back, and looked to be in her 30's to anyone unaware, making many women jealous of her youthfulness.

Hannah grew up between her Chinese father and her American mother. Her father was born and raised in Hong Kong. Hannah often heard of the story of Yoong-Woo Chen, her father, was born to a stable and rich family, and he was sent to the United States to study. Her father's family operated a restaurant in Hong Kong. Once his parents passed away, Hannah's father decided to stay and study abroad in the United States, with just $300 in his possession. After settling down in California, he studied during the day and worked as a dishwasher at night. Hannah's mother Mary Smith, was a fellow art major at the college her father attended. They met there and fell in love. After her father graduated from college, he worked days at the local health clinic and attended classes at night to receive his Masters. They married after his graduation.

Hannah has an older brother and sister. She got along okay with them, although she never felt too close to either of them due to them being much older than her. One spring day, her mother went to the airport to pick up her father from the airport; he had gone to Massachusetts to attend a public medical clinic convention. As she drove them back, they were in a car accident and passed away immediately. Hannah was 20 years old, a third year college student.

Meeting Clint was by complete chance. After her parents passed away, her two other siblings went their separate ways, becoming or working to become independent. Her brother Brian married the woman he was dating, and her sister Anne also married her boyfriend soon after. Hannah kept in contact with her siblings, but for the youngest, Hannah who had suddenly lost both of her parents, loneliness crept up sooner and faster than she had expected. It soon accompanied her everywhere she went. One random day, she had gone to the school library to borrow a book. She held them against her chest and walked down the stairs, but bumped against a male student who was heading into the library. The books fell onto the ground, but as she bent over to pick them up, she tripped on the heels of her shoes and fell, only to have the male student catch her just in the nick of time. That was the first time she realized just how close two people could get. He apologized for his carelessness and introduced himself as Clint. Hannah introduced herself as Hannah Chen. After this brief encounter, they began to spend time each other, getting to know each other better. Clint began to knock at Hannah's shy outer shell, eventually winning her over. They fell in love and dated through college, eventually becoming married.

Hannah would sometimes see a little bit of her father in Clint, seeing them. Hannah couldn't help but feel that this was destiny. The way this began has continued on for the past thirty years, with him being her closest relationship, and not being overstated, but her husband was her best friend. After fifty-five years of life though, she realized one day, that she was beginning to develop a habit of contemplation. Unlike before, her intuition was beginning to take the wheel, and her body would follow, rather than jump in as she used to when she was younger. Hannah had realized that she'd finally crossed the threshold where the time she spent was longer than the time she would spend on this world.

Hannah opened the window. Clear and fresh wind soon filled the room.

Three

Recently, Riverside Community was beginning to see a change; a sleepy community filled with people in their late 50's to 70's. The community began to attract younger generations, waking it from its peaceful sleep and filling it with noise and vibrance.

There is a flat hill called Sweet Hallow a mile to the south of Summerfield, which is located behind Riverside. The hill wrapped around a creek, which made the area amenable to backpackers and other picnickers.

Younger men and women clad in bathing suits and bikinis began to flock towards the road that used to be frequented by the people who reminisced about the yesteryear. Summerfield, which was surrounded by Sweet Hallow, was a popular resort area in Riverside community. People of Riverside would take walks there and get to know their neighbor, usually by passing them on their walks; Hannah and Clint were not the exception. Hannah and Clint also took walks by Summerfield during warmer months of the year. As new neighbors moved in, younger poets began to frequent Café Mundo's Poetry Night, and the music of the café changed from Piano Concerto and Beethoven to chill house genre and other pop music, which provided a new kind of shock to the people of Riverside.

At approximately ten in the morning, Hannah received a phone call from Summer. The past year, Summer hadn't shown up at Poetry Night. Hannah was incredibly concerned with Summer's sudden absence, but realized she knew only her name and nothing else when she decided to look for her. Hannah missed her dearly and was only too happy to hear Summer's voice again, that she was more than willing to jump in the car and drive over to see her. However, Summer stated she was still abroad and would not arrive until the day after. She then asked to meet with Hannah at 3:00 PM on August 9, at the Grishon Café. Grishon Café was at the entrance to Toylor University, and was bustling with college students, despite its larger size in comparison to Café Mundo. It made one think of a school cafeteria than a café, and Hannah hadn't been to the place, so it sounded incredibly out of place for her. But for Hannah, who had missed the regular conversations she'd had with Summer, this distraction would not be a problem.

To Hannah, Summer was Picasso. Her point of view differed from that of the average person, and her thoughts reflected it. Her ability to view multiple points of views and multiple scenarios was like fresh air to Hannah.

Slightly excited, Hannah texted Clint to let him know of her plans to meet with Summer. He must have been busy as reply was a simple "OK" after quite a long time after. As she quietly murmured to herself, "Clint must be very busy," she prepared to meet with Summer.

Because Clint's job took him all over the country, there were only a few states he'd never been to. As a result, Hannah didn't always know where Clint was at any moment, unless he let her know. Even if she called him, she couldn't always reach him.

The road was rather empty as Hannah drove through unfamiliar roads. She then found herself lost for a few minutes, trying to navigate the complicated city roads. After about ten or twenty minutes trying to find a parking spot, she finally managed to get to the café. She opened the door and looked around but couldn't find Summer anywhere. As she glanced around for a familiar face among tall, large students covering her view, someone suddenly grabbed at her arm. The vice-like grip made Hannah wince, but when she looked up at the face connected to the arm, she realized the person as Summer Wu. Hannah forgot her pain and smiled at Summer, but disappeared the moment she looked at Summer's grief-stricken face. Summer brought a finger to her lips and made a quiet "shhhh" sound, and Hannah found herself mimicking Summer's actions. Summer reached down from the arm she was grabbing, then placed a small piece of paper in Hannah's hand, before bringing her lips toward Hannah's ear, and quietly whispered,

"I'm sorry, Hannah. But there's no time! Please!"

Hannah met Summer's desperate eyes, before looking at the piece of paper. It wrapped a small key and had a number written on it. Before Hannah could respond, Summer let go of Hannah's arm and disappeared among the thick mass of students. Hannah felt the wind knocked out of her, as she had expected a nice reunion, but couldn't expect much else after realizing the seriousness of the situation. Hannah pushed through the mass of tall, strong students, found her car, and returned home, all while feeling completely uncomfortable about the situation.

There wasn't much that Hannah knew about Summer. Summer had a home in Richmond Island. She wasn't married, but seemed to be dating. She remembered him as Brent Hammington. The fact that she knew nothing else about Summer made Hannah feel even more uncomfortable. Also, considering the lack of knowledge Hannah had about Summer's life, her behavior seemed to bring about curiosity; did people normally do something like this with people they barely knew?

Four

Summer neared its end, and September came with clearer skies and clouds that seemed to move a bit further away from the world. There was absolutely nothing from Summer, and Hannah had begun to forget about the event that had happened with Summer.

Mr. Ford next door was already out mowing the lawn, at such an early morning too. He was of Native American descent, and had strong pride and self-esteem. However, after he read Hannah's poem, he would kindly answer any questions Hannah might have. His lawn reflected his Native American background, and differed from all of the other yards. A house where the yellow-bellied Robins would stay before flying away, Bluebirds would visit to have a drink and meal, or even humming birds, that even Hannah couldn't help but think of buying a bird house. The neighbors to the left partied almost every night, annoying the quieter residents, who would complain of the nuisance. Hannah began to spend less time at home, choosing instead to go to the local library or take more walks, due to the loud music and bass, and the loud noise of the motorboats of the young couple and their friends, and as the police began to come by more often.

As she opened the refrigerator, Hannah found herself flustered in front of a refrigerator with no ingredients to actually make dinner. It was rather late, and she didn't want to go out. Hannah usually went to the market in the mornings. It was less hot that way, there were less people shopping, and she would forget less things at home because she wouldn't have to hurry. She called Clint, only to hear the voicemail assistant. She left a message,

"I'm going to Riverside Market, so if you happen to be coming home now, and the time is right, let's eat dinner out and shop for food before coming back home together."

She hung up, and changed into suitable clothes to go out. The phone suddenly rang, and it was Clint. Clint let Hannah know that he would be late or possibly not be able to make it home that night, before hanging up.

Hannah hung up and decided to get a few basic items, like bagels and milk, vegetables, beef and pork, before leaving the house. As she drove out, she saw the young couple driving back in. She couldn't help but frown, before driving out of the neighborhood, towards the direction of Riverside Market. She had to pass by Café Mundo on her way; and she saw Summer and Brent get into a car together. It was the first time she'd seen Summer since that incident. Hannah found herself turn into Café Mundo, but a car quickly turned into her lane from the left lane, and she stepped on the break as fast as she could. There was no contact as a result, but when she looked back, Summer and Brent were already gone. Hannah breathed a giant sigh.

She calmed down and drove over to Riverside Market, which was located inside Riverside Shopping Mall. The market was loud and alive, filled with people who'd recently gotten out of work. Hannah shopped without incident and returned home.

She turned the light on the living room on, and washed vegetables before preparing a small salad. She returned to her room and sat in front of the computer. She'd wanted to write a poem about the morning sky she had seen that morning, but she couldn't remember it at all; Summer's strange behavior overtook anything else in her mind. Exactly what had happened to her? Why did she want to meet at Grishon rather than their usual meet-up place, Mundo? Summer's apprehensive eyes and the red mark on Hannah's arm from where Summer had grabbed her overtook her mind completely. She couldn't shake that whatever Summer had given her could actually hold a dangerous meaning; the uneasy apprehension Summer had in her eyes had somehow managed to make its way to Hannah's.

Five

October, 2014, A month Later

Last night in Hannah's dream, Hannah's mother was on a boat, floating down the river, and called out to her. As she'd passed away several decades ago, it gave Hannah an uneasy feeling. Why had she called at Hannah? Hannah had gone to sleep early morning, but woke up once more, and she was surprised to find the clarity in her mind. Her restless mind eventually forced her out of bed, and into the living room, where she paced back and forth with different thoughts. She eventually came to the conclusion that she'd prepare breakfast for Clint, since he'd soon wake up. She blended some tomatoes into juice and prepared a simple sandwich. A little while after, half-asleep Clint woke up with peculiar look on his face. Hannah was a night owl, yet here she was, fully awake. After she sent off Clint for the day, Clint still dealing with the unusualness of the situation with shaking of his head, she found her mind becoming cloudier than before. It was still quite early, but the Sun was coming up, so she decided to air out the house before going back to bed and opened the window. The river was filled with fog, which made the whole scene look utterly surreal as the fog writhed on the top of the river. The world seen with a tired mind seemed like that of a dream.

The Sun wasn't the only thing waking up in the morning. As the fog began to dissipate with the warmth of sunlight, and the sunlight washed over the river, a group of geese could be seen preening and going through the tall grass growing on the side of the river. Suddenly, the geese flew away, as if caught by surprise. Hannah picked up the telescope to look at what had interrupted their peaceful morning, and almost fell and fainted when she came upon the sight. A person was lying among the grasses. Hannah could only see the back of the woman from her angle. She seemed to be barefooted, with black chiffon dress barely showing her knees. The sight of blood around her seemed to explain what had happened. Hannah couldn't look much more; she was frozen with fear and was jolted to life when Clint called her.

"Don't forget to send off the car tax payments today. The bills are on my desktop, next to the computer."

"I… I got it, but… What do I do?!" Hannah's voice shook with each word, and she couldn't say much more afterwards. Clint's voice, full of frustration, asked her to speak up.

"There seems to be a corpse by the riverbed, in the river grass. She's not moving! She must be dead! I'm so scared, I can't go down to check!"

"What? What are you… Call the police and report it! What are you doing?! Call them right now!"

"O… Okay, I will…" and she hung up.

As soon as she came to, she called 911.

"911, this is Nate. What's the emergency?" a voice similar to the automatic voice system could be heard from the opposite side, Hannah had to explain herself thoroughly. She explained that from where she was at home, there was a person on the riverbed, who didn't seem to be moving.

Hannah said, "Hello, my name is Hannah Walter. I live on Riverside Drive in Pork Rock City. I opened the window to clean this morning, and found a woman by the riverbed. She's not moving. I think she may be dead. Please hurry!"

"Okay, we will send someone out." Said the man's voice across from the line.

Even after hanging up, Hannah couldn't take her eyes off-of the telescope. What if she got back up and starts walking again, or maybe a boat crashed and she floated in? She didn't know, but she couldn't move away. Whose blood was it? If someone stabbed or shot her, there should have been some noise, yet there was nothing last night. What had happened? The riverbed was only about fifteen feet from her house... she waited, million thoughts running through her mind, she was frozen at her spot, waiting for the police.

The thought of airing out the house and going back to sleep had long gone from her mind, and she felt wide awake. She'd check once in a while for some sign of people while looking outside, and jumped when someone rang on her doorbell.

The police, ambulance, and even the fire truck arrived at the neighborhood, causing much noise and chaos. Neighbors whose names were unknown would come out to glance at Hannah's house, curious as to the reason for all of the ruckus. Hannah explained how she found the body, by showing them the location of the telescope and where the body was. One of the older gentlemen, who identified himself as Detective Jameson looked at her in a way that unnerved her. He glanced over the messy desk, filled with manuscript pages, or unfinished poems, before noting,

"It seems your desk is very messy."

Hannah blinked a couple of times, as if broken from a trance, realizing that the detective was speaking to her, and nodded.

"Yes, I do."

"What are you writing?"

"I'm an author."

"So you work from home?"

"Yes, I do."

Detective Jameson rubbed at his beard, staring at her in a discerning way that unnerved her earlier. Her brown eyes and his icy blue eyes met. She rubbed at her arm, trying to get rid of the sudden chill running down her spine. Jameson's eagle-like eyes then went to her arms, before coming back to her face. He gave her a smile, but she could tell his smile wasn't reaching his eyes.

"I understand you're shocked, but to get you off the suspect list, I need to ask you a couple of questions. And... I'll need you to come down to the station and get fingerprints done. It's all procedural things, so don't worry."

Hannah panicked at Detective. Jameson's words. Her face became filled with discomfort, and paled at the idea of going to the police station, which she never had to do before.

"Po... police station?! But... I haven't done anything wrong!"

Det. Jameson replied mechanically,

"As you are the first witness, and as you're the caller, I simply need to get some more information from you."

Hannah eventually agreed to follow Det. Jameson to the station. He said that it was important to get this done while her memory was still fresh, and Hannah wanted to get this out of her mind as fast as she could, so she promised to follow him. The lack of a phone call from her husband was unnerving, but she wasn't the criminal. She was simply going in as a witness.

Soon after, the medics brought the bloodied woman on a stretcher, and she had the oxygen mask and IV's attached to her. Because there were so many things attached on her, Hannah couldn't see the woman's face, but she was glad to see that they hadn't covered her face up, and gave a relieved sigh. Now that such matter was complete, Hannah couldn't help but be nervous at the idea of having to go to the police station.

The ambulance left the neighborhood with a loud siren, and the people around her were talking amongst themselves, but she couldn't hear any of them. She thought Mr. Ford from next door was calling her, but she couldn't even think to look his way. She was simply getting too shocked and too tired to understand the events of the morning. It was a little later that she realized her heart was beating faster than normal, due to the nightmare-like reality unfolding before her.

Six

In front of Hannah was a two-story concrete building. The front said "Riverside Police Station," and had the US flag and the New York State flag flying to the left. Hannah entered the lot, which was filled with patrol cars, parked her Volkswagen Beetle in the Visitor's spot, and followed Det. Jameson into the building.

Her body felt like soaked sponge, although her mind couldn't detect fatigue due to the shock from the events in the morning. The detective had offered to drive her, but for Hannah, who'd always believed only criminals got in patrol cars, it was a scary offer. Hannah told him she'd follow him and did so.

She didn't want to follow a cop anywhere, but didn't want him to confirm whatever suspicion he might have had of her. Without turning on even the radio, she'd followed him carefully. Hannah couldn't look around, fearful that everyone around was staring at her. She felt like the accused although she hadn't done anything wrong.

When she'd arrived, she didn't dare muster up the courage to walk in by herself. The police station looked so foreign and imposing, like those she saw in movies.

Det. Jameson finally arrived, walking toward Hannah. His tough walking style and straight back seemed to reflect his dry and picky personality perfectly.

"Here you are, Ms. Walter. Let's go in. It won't take long."

Hannah merely swallowed, unable to say anything else, and followed him in. The office was surprisingly quieter than expected. A woman in her early twenties in navy uniform was sitting. Her uniform had the "City of Riverside Police" embroidered on, and a name "Ashley Simpson" on it.

She looked at Hannah and the detective and merely nodded. Hannah felt even more insecure.

"Ashley," said the detective, "This is Hannah Walter. She was the witness that called in about the possible death incident at Pork Rock. Go ahead and get her prints done and send her into my room when she's done."

Ashley Simpson replied that she would, and took Hannah to a smaller room to the side. The room was rather small, only about the size of her walk-in closet in the master bedroom at home. The small room was filled with copier and other office supplies. She rubbed her fingers onto a black ink pad and pressed each finger onto a piece of paper with labels of the fingers on them. She then said,

"Since you have deep fingerprints, you probably shouldn't commit any crimes."

Upon seeing Hannah's frozen face, Ashley said,

"I'm just joking! You're too nervous! Don't worry so much; this is just procedure to clear any witnesses off of the suspect list, so don't worry."

After all her fingers turned black with ink, and the white paper were filled with her prints, Ashley handed her a towel, and Hannah wiped off the ink on her hands. As she stared at the ink smudges on the towel, she couldn't help but feel lightheaded. What was she doing there? She'd realized then, that she was truly regretting her finding out of the incident today. It was annoying, and she couldn't help but feel horribly annoyed about it. At least for that moment, she hated Clint for rubbing his hobby onto Hannah; had he not had such an annoying hobby, she wouldn't have seen anything.

After her hands were clean, Ashley took her to Det. Jameson's office. She knocked on his door, and soon, he replied, "Come in," with his emotionless voice.

Detective Jameson offered her the seat across from him, and she sat down. Detective Jameson's desk was filled with papers and books, and reports with paper clips on them, all lined up and organized. It was the exact opposite of hers back home.

Det. Jameson gave her a simple explanation.

"First of all, I just wanted to let you know that I did not call you in on any suspicion or to charge you of a crime. I want you to remember that you're a witness here to help us find the real perpetrator."

Hannah pushed her body inward compared with earlier, when she was sitting just at the tip.

"Yes, okay, I understand."

Unlike before, Hannah's face relaxed slightly. Seeing this, Det. Jameson began to talk,

"How did you come upon the body?"

"I have a habit of opening the door to the deck every morning to air out the house. Like today, I also have a habit of looking through the telescope. When I looked at the movement of geese by my house rather than across the river this morning, I happened to see her body."

"Did you say you look across the river with your telescope?"

"Yes. My husband and I have a hobby of watching the night sky with telescope. I have a habit of looking out at the river in the morning and observing the life around it."

"Do you also look at your neighbors with that telescope?"

Hannah couldn't answer right away.

"I never intended to watch them, but they would come within the vicinity of the lens sometimes."

"If that's the case, was there something strange or different about this morning, that you normally don't see?"

"Not really. If anything, it were the geese that found her amongst the weeds,"

"Geese?"

"Yes."

Det. Jameson stopped for a second to touch his beard. Hannah looked at him carefully. He then stopped and looked back at Hannah.

"When did you actually see the body?"

"I think… Around seven or seven-thirty in the morning."

"Don't you know the exact time?"

"I woke up a little wary today. After my husband left for work, I was going to air out the house and go to sleep."

"You woke up early today?"

"Earlier than usual, yes."

"Then, did you hear something like a woman's scream or a sound of a gun?"

Hannah shook her head.

"No, I did not hear anything."

"What time did you wake up today?"

"Around 3 A.M."

"What time do you normally wake up at?"

"Around 7 to 8."

"Why did you wake up so early today?"

Hannah stammered briefly.

"I had a nightmare."

"So you were home the whole time?"

"Yes, that is right."

"Since it was still early, you didn't go anywhere else either?"

"No, I was in the kitchen preparing my husband's breakfast."

He seemed to believe her only halfway; Hannah was also filled with self critical thoughts. Why out of all days, did she wake up earlier than usual *today*?

He then simply asked,

"If I ask your husband, he'll vouch for your whereabouts?"

"Yes."

"Does he know what you were doing between three and seven in the morning today?"

"He… was asleep."

"I see. That'll be all for today. If it's all right, may I have your and your husband's name and contact information? If there is new information or question, I'll contact you."

Hannah got up to shake his outstretched hand. His hand was dry and rough. His handshake was exact and controlled.

As soon as she left Det. Jameson's office, her eyes met Ashley's, who was by the door. She smiled and gave a little nod. Hannah replicated, and wanted to smile, but her nervousness refused to relax the muscles on her face, preventing her from giving a smile back.

On the way back, Hannah could feel her mind becoming even cloudier. She wasn't a criminal. Det. Jameson's questions though, made her feel as if she were related to the case somehow, and his words made her feel uncomfortable. They messed with her mind even more.

After returning from the station, she could feel the onset of tiredness setting in, but didn't have the heart to go back home. She was scared. The fear of finding someone else dying by the river behind her house, fear of someone who knew she was the witness and came after her, or even the possibility of someone breaking into her house and waiting for her to come back… fear created endless scenarios in Hannah's head, spread out like her desk. Eventually, she gave up on going back home. She went to the one hotel in Riverside and checked in. It was a bit worn, but for that one moment, she felt safe.

She lied down on the slightly scratchy bed, and when she did, she could feel her body relaxing; for a while, nothing but the sound of the air conditioning and the sound of her quiet breathing could be heard.

She didn't know how long she was sleeping, but she woke to her cellphone ringing. It was Clint, and it was already eight at night. Jolted awake, she quickly picked up the phone.

"Where are you?! Why didn't you pick up the phone until now?!"

"I'm sorry, Clint. I couldn't possibly go home... so I'm staying at the hotel."

Clint's relieved sigh over the phone made her realize she'd forgotten to call him back after everything had happened that day. Clint then said,

"I came back to an empty house. I even hurried home because I was worried."

"I'm sorry, Clint. There wasn't... anyone at home, or ...something off, was there?"

"Of course not. Why? You don't feel like coming home?"

"No, I don't. Can you... bring your and my clothes and come over here? I don't think I could sleep there tonight."

Clint said yes, and hung up the phone. After about twenty minutes, he appeared with a small bag, and made clucking noise with the tongue in disapproval.

"You should have picked a better hotel... it looks more dangerous here."

Hannah explained, "I was so tired, I just chose whatever I could find."

Clint pulled at Hana's arm and said, "No, this won't do. We can't sleep here, even if it's the only hotel in town. Let's go."

As they left the room and paid, a black sedan with dark tint passed by them. Since there were many rich people living in Riverside, it shouldn't have looked all the special, but Hannah couldn't help but feel a shiver go down her spine as the car passed by. But once she got on Clint's 2006 Volvo, her memory of the black car soon dissipated.

The two went into Riverside Best Hotel's parking lot by Toylor University, and went into the hotel. Although it was late, there was an empty room. They took their card key and went over to the elevator to get to room 7011. When the elevator arrived, they got in, and Clint pressed 7. There was another man who entered the elevator. Hannah didn't think much until she realized that someone was staring at her. She realized he was looking at her rather than at Clint. She looked up at him, and he gave a small smile before using his right hand to push the hair out of his face. The ring on his finger sparkled brightly. Hannah couldn't help but feel that she'd met this person before. She began to think about where she'd seen him before. When they arrived on the seventh floor, Clint pulled Hannah's hand, and the two began to go further away from the man in the elevator.

As soon as she reached the room with Clint, Hannah began to feel reassured that no one was following them. Clint called for room service, pulled off his jacket, and hung it in the closet. He then went into shower. Hannah lied on the soft king sized bed and looked up at the ceiling. She was less tired than before, and could think clearly about the events that had occurred today, but she couldn't really pick out anything special or different from before. She'd seen a nearly dead person for the first time in her life, and had been to the police station. She had her fingerprints done and was questioned by a detective. She hadn't slept properly, and she'd never been this afraid since her parents passed away.

Soon after, Clint came out, wrapped in a towel, and pulled out his underwear from the overnight bag, and put it on. There was a small chair and table, and a sofa in the king-sized bedroom. Hannah could feel her body feel shaky and sticky, and walked into the bathroom with underwear and pajamas. She decided she needed a bath rather than a shower tonight. After the bell rang, a cart filled with food came into the room. Hotel employee set the room up with food and left. Clint thanked and tipped him, as the employee said, "Please enjoy the food," and left the room.

After Hannah came back out of the bathroom, she saw the food Clint ordered on the table. Clint was sitting by the table, waiting for her. There was Hannah's favorite, lobster with lemon on top of the table. The fresh smell of lemon permeated throughout the room, and the lobster was still very warm, as she could see the steam coming up from it. But, as soon as she grabbed at the lobster to eat, she could feel her appetite disappear, as discomfort set in. Why couldn't she hear anything although she was awake at that hour?

Normally, she'd enjoy the food, but the thoughts floating in her mind prevented her from enjoying the food. The complicated thoughts made her lose her appetite.

Clint seemed to notice her complicated thoughts, and lied on the bed after dinner, telling her to sleep since it was a tiring day. He was of course, tired, and Hannah was also mentally exhausted. He soon fell asleep, but she couldn't, lying awake. She realized the man she'd seen at the hotel lobby and the elevator recognized her. Who was he?

Seven

Clint eventually ended up calling in for a day off in the morning. As soon as he received the okay from his superior, he fell back to bed. After all, he hadn't had a proper meets or vacation for the past seven years, focused entirely on work. After a while, he got up and opened the window curtains and looked out at the river, before saying to Hannah,

"You've never crossed that river before, right? After breakfast, do you want to go check it out?"

"I've never been, but what if the bridge raises up and we can't leave and come back?"

"We won't be there for too long."

"Okay. Let's do it, then."

Clint and Hannah went downstairs to the hotel restaurant, had a simple breakfast before coming back to the room. Clint turned the TV on as soon as they returned to the room and lied sideways on the bed. The 9 o'clock news happened to be on.

"The identity of the person found On the South Bay river in Pork Rock at approximately 10 o'clock yesterday morning has yet to be found. She is currently in critical condition at a hospital in Riverside. If anyone can give information on her identity, please contact the Riverside police. She is an Asian-American in her thirties."

"Asian and in her thirties?" Hannah rubbed down her arm, fear suddenly rearing its ugly head once more.

Clint must have dozed off, as he asked with a voice filled with sleep, "huh?" But Hannah merely shook her head and told him to rest. She then closed the window curtains and went back to be and lied down next to Clint.

As she was tossing and turning due to a restless mind, she still felt tired and heavy. She crawled back into the comforter. She couldn't tell how long she'd been asleep. Someone knocked on the door, and she opened the door to find the hotel maid. As she cleaned the room, Clint asked Hannah of she wanted to stay another night, but Hannah told him she'd go back home, and they gathered their belongings before checking out of the hotel.

They went to "Beijing," a Chinese buffet restaurant in the area. Hannah still couldn't find much appetite and ate little. Clint, as usual, went back and forth, eating and returning to the buffet several times. Even during lunch, Hannah couldn't help but feel that someone was looking at her. She looked about but did not meet the eyes of anyone particular or find a suspicious individual. Because she was rather immobile, wrapped by fear, and Clint tended to bring her food, telling her to have some.

After lunch, they crossed the bridge and onto the entrance point onto Richmond Island, which was the envy of all those living in Riverside. There was a small security point at the entryway. Left, right, and center. The island was divided by three main roads separating the island. The guard told them to stop the car. Clint stopped the car. He asked for an ID and where they were going. Clint showed him the ID and told him that he loved across the river and wanted to visit the area and had the time to do so today. The guard told him to turn around and leave as the island had a list of approved cars, which were the only ones allowed on the island apart from the residents. Clint turned the car around, and grabbed onto Hannah's hand as he wordlessly drove back out. As they returned home, he only stared ahead, as if he'd forgotten how to speak.

As soon as they arrived, Hannah locked the door by the balcony facing the river and closed it with a double-thick curtain. The room darkened immediately. Clint must have left the house in a hurry as the bedroom light was still on.

Clint went into the study, opened the computer, and began to work in preparation for tomorrow. Hannah made a warm cup of tea and brought it to his desk. As she left the tea and tried to leave, he grabbed Hannah's hand.

"Don't worry, hon. No matter what happens, I'll protect you."

"Yeah... thank you."

"I'm being serious. Don't you trust me?"

"I... do."

"It seems as if you're unsure..."

"No... well... is... is it okay if you spend the day with me instead of... working? You're taking the day off and all..."

Clint turned the computer off and left the study on Hannah's request. Although the house was darker than usual for the time of the day, he said nothing.

"Would you like to buy a thicker curtain?" asked Clint.

Hannah shook her head, "No... it's all right," and answered back.

Two of them sat on the sofa, but they felt as if they were living completely isolated from the rest of the world. Clint gave a short sigh and eventually picked up the remote control. He turned the TV and began to shift through the channels. Hannah silently accepted his breaking of the silence.

Every time he pressed the remote, another channel popped up. Clint continued to change the channel and stopped at local news.

It was marked as breaking news and had the words "Woman at South Bay River Identified" in red letters, with a greying plump man in a navy police officer uniform standing in front of a group of reporters. Behind him was Detective Jameson.

"The victim in the hospital was identified as a 37-year old newspaper reporter, Summer Wu. We are still investigating how she was found by the riverbed, and will report as the case progresses."

Hannah realized she had gotten off of the sofa unwittingly and was standing in front of the TV. Clint was still sitting on the sofa, but his face also betrayed calm.

"Hey, that woman, isn't she the reporter that comes to your Poetry night?"

Clint remembered her.

Hannah could say nothing, and merely nodded. She was having a difficult time due to the shock yesterday, but to know that the victim was her friend Summer, the one she felt a close connection to all these time made her feel as if her heart had dropped to her stomach.

"I can't believe what's happened."

"She was healthy the last time we met... how..."

"You met her? When?"

Hannah then remembered she hadn't told him about meeting Summer at the café by Toylor University. She had to explain it to him.

"A few months ago, I met Summer by the Toylor University café... although it was for a brief moment."

"How?"

Then Hannah remembered everything, "Summer was... weird. At first, I didn't even know she was in the café. Then she appeared out of nowhere, gave me a key, and disappeared."

"Have you seen her since then?"

"No. But I saw her get into a car with a man in front of Mundo."

The two quieted down once more. There was nothing but the sound of the television left in the living room.

"If you know her, shouldn't you go visit her at the hospital?"

"The broadcast said it was a hospital in Riverside, but which one is it?"

"There aren't that many hospitals in Riverside that could treat someone with such a horrible injury."

"It's probably... Pork Rock or Riverside."

Clint got up from the sofa and walked to the kitchen. A little while later, he came back with two cups of woolong tea and handed her a cup while sipping from his own.

"Do you want to you go now? I'll drive." He gulped down the rest of his woolong tea and got up to get his car keys, but Hannah grabbed his arm to stop him.

"Don't worry, I'll take care of it."

"But to think the victim is someone you know… are you sure you'll be okay? I think this is a bit risky… your face is pale."

"I'm fine… not even…"

Hannah shook her head as she got off of the sofa, and Clint sat back down with a grunt. She tapped his knee a few times, and walked into the kitchen. And she decided to prepare dinner for the first time in a while. Since he usually ate dinner out, she'd not had to cook much. They ate out during the weekend, so there wasn't much need to use the kitchen at all these days. Hannah cooked Clint's favorite food, steamed fish, and Clint ate happily, talking about how much he had missed her food. Looking at Clint's happy face, Hannah was able to forget, even for a little bit, the events that had occurred the past couple of days.

They turned in early, as Clint and Hannah went back to bed. Hannah lied down, using Clint's arm as her pillow. They realized they'd been away from each other for a very long time. Clint gave Hannah a warm embrace. As they lied there quietly, they realized they were like any other couple in their fifties, living through shaking winds and a reed in their hearts.

Hannah woke up early the next day again. Clint went to work, although he worried about her the whole time, and Hannah walked back and forth, trying to get some housework done. She tried, but couldn't do anything.

Without being able to complete the housework, Hannah thought of Summer, who must still be lying in the hospital bed. She had to see Summer. The last time they'd met, she was already in danger. Why hadn't she known?

Eight

It was a perfectly normal autumn day, with clear sky, cool breeze, and bright sunlight. But to Hannah, the sky outside of the window seemed dreary. It was a blue sky just like yesterday and the day before. Two days ago, Hannah found an unconscious, severely injured woman by the riverbed, and yesterday, she found out that person was Summer.

She decided to go see Summer. Hannah worried about her state, and also couldn't hold in the curiosity behind the key she remembered of again. Hannah happened to come across the key while searching through the jacket she wore that day and brought it out to the living room. She turned the key back and forth and stared at it intensely with her hand, the other hand supporting her chin, trying to figure out what could be so special about it. In the end, it was just a plain key. It would be difficult to find her, let alone go see her though. She didn't know anyone who worked at the hospital, and because she wasn't Summer's family member, no one could help her gain entry into the room with a crime victim in critical condition.

She opened the day with a cup of coffee and a bagel with extra strawberry cream cheese spread. She took a sip, then a bite of the bagel, and then another sip of the coffee.

As she ate breakfast and contemplated what to do, the phone rang.

"Is this Hannah Walter?"

"Yes, that's me."

"Hello, I am Detective Jameson. I am in charge of this investigation. We've met before."

The emotionless and businesslike tone. She couldn't forget the voice of the man who'd unnerved others with a sharp wit and dagger-like questioning, and who'd made her feel as if she were a criminal; the man who could transfer his stiffness to others: Detective Jameson. Hannah replied back, carefully.

"Yes. Hello."

"Are you all right?"

"Well… yes… more or less."

"That's good. I just wanted to update you on our findings up to now."

"Okay."

"First, there was no trace of your fingerprint on the victim's body."

"Okay."

"As you may have seen on the TV, the victim's name is Summer Wu."

"Yes. I've also watched the TV."

"Have you heard of her before?"

"… of course…"

"If you've read the Gazette, of course you'd know her name."

"Well… yes."

"But to my knowledge, you know Summer Wu personally."

Hannah felt her heart fall. The hand grabbing onto her phone began to shake ever so slightly, and the beat of her heart rang inside her ears. Hannah breathed deeply. She tried to calm herself, telling herself that this was what detectives did.

"How did you know?" Hannah's voice didn't shake.

"After I looked up information regarding Summer Wu, your name came up. Do you know her personally?"

"Yes, I do."

"You met her at Café Mundo, right?"

"Yes."

"Was she your friend?"

"I think we're still friends... what do you mean by 'was'?"

"Ah, I apologize. My mistake. As expected of an author; you're quite exact in your wording."

"If you have anything else to ask, let me know. I'll answer them. But I also would like some help from you."

"I cannot guarantee that I could help you with whatever you need... but let's hear it anyway."

"I would like to know what hospital Summer Wu is at. I'd like to go see her in the hospital."

"That's a bit difficult..."

"Then I will no longer feel obligated to answer you. I didn't harm Summer."

"I see. I will do what I can."

"Okay."

"Then let me ask you just one more question today. Before you found Ms. Wu in front of your river, did you meet or see her?"

She was surprised at the same line of questioning Det. Jameson had as her husband Clint. She began to feel more uneasy, as if she was caught in something way more complicated.

"Yes. I met her a few months back at Grishon Café. After that... I saw her once more in passing in front of Café Mundo. She was with a man at the time, and she got into the car with him."

"A man?" Det. Jameson asked.

"Yes. I think he was quite young." Hannah answered truthfully.

"Do you happen to remember what he looked like?"

"Hm... I'm not sure..." Hannah hesitated. She tried to remember but came up with nothing.

"What did you discuss at Grishon Café?"

"To be honest... nothing special. I'm not sure you could really call it as a meeting or anything like that. I hadn't seen her in months, and then she called me one day from abroad. Then... we agreed to meet at Grishon..." and Hannah hesitated once more. She wasn't sure she should tell him everything.

"And. ?"

"We didn't get to drink even a cup of coffee before we went our ways that day. We didn't get to talk at all." Hannah didn't say anything about the key. Since he hadn't asked, she didn't think she was obligated to answer.

"Was there anything different about her behavior? Det. Jameson's questions kept continuing. Hannah's nervousness deep-end the dark shadow cast over the gloomy mood of the house.

"To be honest with you, she was a bit different than normal. It seemed... as if she were being chased."

"I see." Det. Jameson replied, "If there is any new development, I will contact you. And..." He hesitated, "If I can find information on where Ms. Wu is, I'll call you." And he hung up.

Hannah sat in the quiet living room, and stared at the cold cup of coffee and half-eaten bagel. She realized she wouldn't be able to relax at home today, and prepared to get out.

Summer's current state, curiosity behind the key, and everything that'd started... Hannah realized she would find no answers at home, and placed the key deep inside her purse. She locked the front door and got into the car. As she turned the engine on and left, she never saw the black sedan with tinted windows parked on the opposite side of the house.

Nine

Hannah showed the key to the owner of the keysmith in the mall.

"Hm…" The keysmith turned the key back and forth, and replied,

"This doesn't seem like your regular house key."

"Really?" Hannah asked back,

"It's too small to be a house key, and the grooves wouldn't fit your average door. It's also not the size of a key for a safe you keep in a house."

Hannah thanked the man and left the store. As she drove her car out of the mall, she fell into thought. It confirmed her beliefs that this was no ordinary key. She visited many of the keysmiths but they all answered the same. It wasn't a house key.

Even if she knew that, Hannah still couldn't quite figure out what else this was supposed to open, and she couldn't help but fall into worry. She'd hit the wall from the beginning, and her chest felt tight from the lack of progress. She thought about calling that detective, but decided that a person who wouldn't even keep his part of the bargain shouldn't be trusted. It didn't take that long to figure out where Summer was, after all. She had to find another way. Hannah then decided to have lunch at Café Mundo for a late lunch. She opened the door and entered. Then she froze.

There was the man she'd seen with Summer, wiping tables inside the Café. His face and the face in her memory matched, and her heart skipped beats, before ramming against her ribcage. She sat down at the nearby empty table, and began to observe him quietly. For Hannah, who wrote for a living, observing people's behavior and expressions was second nature. Her eyes followed him easily, looking at his movements, facial expressions whenever he talked, and the way he carried himself. He didn't seem that worried. As he talked with a woman who seemed to be a patron, he would cackle, leaning against the bar, and exchanging glances with the woman. Hanna had seen him get into a car with Summer, yet how could he be here, nonchalantly, working? Hannah's eyes never left him, as questions gave birth to more questions in her head. Finally, he must have felt Hannah's glances, as he said something to the woman, and with a more professional face, walked over to Hannah. She looked at his chest. On a black button down shirt was a name tag "Brandon."

"Wecome to Café Mundo. I'm Brandon. What would you like to order today?" He sat down a menu in front of Hannah.

"Hi… Brandon. I'd like Lunch menu no. 4." Hannah ordered without looking at the menu.

He took down the order in his notepad and asked while looking back at her,

"What would you like for a drink?"

"I'll take an iced green tea."

"Will do!" Brandon then walked back into the kitchen. Hannah quietly stared at him as he walked away. About ten minutes later, Brandon brought the iced green tea on top of a round tray, and brought it to Hannah before placing it on her table. She took a sip. It was cool. It softened Hannah's mind, split and dry like late autumn. As she found herself relaxing unlike earlier, she decided to organize everything that'd happened so far. She pulled out a notebook that she always carried, and wrote down important date and time, related persons, location, and related information, but couldn't find much of a link between them. She felt that she was missing something important, but couldn't figure out what that was nor could she remember anything.

Ten minutes after, Brandon brought out her lunch. Hannah took a bite of the warm Italian sandwich and took a fork to the cobb salad before taking a bite of it. As she ate, Mundo's owner, Ashley walked out.

"Hannah!" Ashley rushed over, seemingly happy to see her.

"It's been awhile, Ashley." Hannah swallowed the food and said a simple hello.

"Can you believe something like this would happen around here? To Summer of all people!" Ashley was also concerned with what had happened to Summer.

"Hm…" Hannah took another sip of the iced tea and answered nonchalantly, "Indeed…, I would like to go see her, but I don't know where she is… there's no information on that… I really don't know what to do."

"I understand…" Ashley sat on the opposite chair to Hannah. She rested her chin on her right hand and continued to talk, "everyone who'd been coming to Poetry Night had been wondering where Summer had gone; to think she'd reappear like this…"

Hannah nodded. Hannah couldn't possibly tell Ashley that she'd been the one to find Summer's injured body. When she remembered her blood-soacked body, she couldn't take another bite.

"Ah,… so…" Hannah began slowly, "you got a new waiter."

"Yes," Ashley answered, "His name is Brandon; used to go to the Toylor University Law School, but dropped out… something about law being the wrong field…" Ashley then called Brandon over.

"Can you get me a cup of water, Brandon?" Brandon smiled and nodded, before preparing a cup of water and coming over to where Hannah and Ashley were sitting.

"Here you are, Ashley."

"Thanks." Ashley took a sip of water, and engaged Brandon once more.

"This is Hannah Walter. She's our star of Poetry Night." Brandon smiled even more once he heard her name.

"So you're Hannah Walter. I really enjoyed your poems. I had an exam the next day, but couldn't stop bawling the night before!" Brandon was incredibly extraverted and social.

He grabbed her hand tightly and shook it, and as Hannah felt his rather warm hand, couldn't help but think that youngsters were different. She gave him a polite smile, and Brandon smiled, all of his teeth showing.

He asked Ashley if he could use his break now, and Ashley agreed. Since it was a late afternoon, there weren't many people around. He brought a chair and sat on another corner. He then began to talk to Hannah.

"I've been meaning to attend this week's Poetry Night. After reading your poem, I decided law wasn't my route anymore, and decided to write instead! I actually hold more than one part-time jobs right now, so I've not been able to make time, but I am definitely planning to attend tomorrow night! Will you be there as well?"

"Ah… well… that is the plan, yes." Hannah felt herself falling into his pace. It felt risky. She had to cure her curiosity. She decided to be courageous.

"By some chance… did you…" She brought up the subject.

"Yes?"

"Do you know Summer Wu?"

"Summer Wu? Who was that… it seems familiar…" Brandon was hesitant in answering. Hannah could feel her temper rise up quickly. What situation was this?

"Surely… you do watch the news, right? How could you NOT know Summer Wu?" Ashley answered for him.

"I didn't say I didn't know her. I just couldn't remember her momentarily. Ah, that Summer Wu. Well, if I didn't know *that* Summer Wu in this area right now, everyone would think I was an idiot. Of course I do." Brandon smiled and agreed.

"Before… I was on my way somewhere and saw you and her get into the same car." Hannah confessed truthfully. Brandon didn't even blink.

"Ah, yes. To be honest, I do remember going on a date with her once. I was still attending law school at the time, and someone I knew introduced her to me, but we didn't find any similarities, so we didn't see each other since then." Brandon answered. Hannah saw his eyes, which seemed to be truthful, and realized she'd made a mistake. She apologized.

"I'm sorry. I made a rude mistake as I've been very worried about Summer."

Brandon merely shrugged and replied, "Well, if I'd seen Summer Wu with you before she got injured, I would have also considered it suspicious." Then he continued, "If you're that uncomfortable… since it's nearly dinner time, would you buy me dinner? I've been breaking my back trying to pay off law school loans, so I've been pretty much broke!" She agreed to a still smiling man. Ashley, Brandon, and Hannah discussed continuously for hours until very late evening.

Hannah returned home after spending half the day at Café Mundo. As she came into the driveway, she realized the front door was completely open, and quickly turned off the ignition, running towards the front door. She looked about the area and saw nothing extraordinary.

She quickly rummaged through her purse to find the cell phone, and with shaky fingers, dialed 911. "Emergency Service. What's the name and address?" a slightly low-toned female answered the phone. Hannah told her the name and address, then, "It seems like someone broke into my house! The front door is completely open! I'm not sure if anyone else is in the house, so I haven't entered yet!" explained the situation.

"Okay. In that case, it's probably good that you didn't go into the house. Is there anywhere nearby you can be safe in?" She asked. Hannah looked around and saw her car.

"Just my car."

"Then, please wait there. I will send someone over."

"Yes. Please hurry!"

Hannah hung up her cell phone and locked the car door once she returned to it. To think, Summer's discovery a few days back, and a break-in at her house today, the drama of it all made it difficult for her to understand. Where and why had it gone wrong?

The police appeared about an hour after. He first went in through the main door, turned the light on, and came out to let Hannah know of the situation.

"It doesn't seem like anyone is in there, so let me look around for prints or evidence. Just wait out here."

"I understand," replied Hannah, and sat back down in her car.

The police wrapped the house with yellow "Do not Enter" tape, and took plastic gloves and shoe cover into the house as they searched for prints and evidence. Hannah couldn't control the overwhelming fear growing inside this nightmare. Then she remembered. Clint didn't know anything about this. It was already seven o'clock at night. Hannah quickly called Clint, and a surprised Clint replied he would head straight home and hung up. Hannah looked at the house with glazed eyes. Unlike the afternoon, it had become significantly colder, and Hannah rubbed at her arms and shivered.

"Well, well... unfortunate things seem to keep happening to and around you these days," said a low voice behind her. Hannah and the police officer who'd been nearby asking her questions looked to find Det. Jameson. The police officer gave Jameson a simple acknowledgement, and Jameson reciprocated before he walked toward Hannah.

"To be honest... I didn't think I'd see you this early already. Are you all right?"

Hannah nodded, "Thank you for coming, detective."

Det. Jameson, with a simple nod, went into the house.

"I don't think this is your average crime. Ms. Walter... please tell me. Have you received a threat or seen someone suspicious lately?"

Hannah shook her head, "I didn't see anyone particularly suspicious."

Det. Jameson wrote a few things down, and directed someone to take a few photos. Clint arrived, but the two didn't leave the front of the house and stood there, simply holding hands. When the police left, it was already early morning, but Hannah and Clint hugged each other tightly as they went to sleep on the same bed, unable to go to a nearby hotel from the ever-growing fear.

46

Ten

Summer's Dead. Hannah never met Summer again after discovering her body that day. She'd bothered Det. Jameson about it over the phone, but the detective only replied,

"I've also made inquiry with the hospital, but they said only family were allowed. Also, as Ms. Summer Wu was still in a coma, unless she says she wants to see you, there isn't much else I can do. If she wakes up, I'll ask her about you and help you get things arranged, so you can go see her."

But that day never came. She'd been deemed stable, yet was found dead the next day, on her hospital bed, by a nurse. It was a few days ago. On the front cover of the Gazette's obituary was a big picture of Summer, and her notable works. Funeral was to be a week from that day, and Hannah decided she'd go there no matter what'd happened. The last time she'd seen Summer alive was at the parking lot of Mundo, as Hannah had drove past her, but she wanted to see her off before Summer took her last long trip.

Everything felt like a dream. Maybe a cheap drama. Except for losing her parents at an early age, Hannah had lived a normal life for the past fifty years, and the events of the past few days felt so out of place and ridiculous. They all seemed to be related somehow, yet not all of the puzzle pieces were there, and she didn't understand what kind of a puzzle she was putting in either. Who would benefit from the completion of the puzzle, or how things would move forward from then on; none of them made sense. But Hannah felt something from deep within. She didn't know what it was, but she would be the one to finish it. That this was going to be very dangerous.

Week went by in a flash, and Hannah and Clint drove over to the park cemetery in Sweet Hallow. The place was filled with people in black. Summer was Riverside's best newspaper, Gazette's lead reporter, so it made sense. Everyone's face was filled with confusion and sadness, but Hannah's eyes landed on an old couple and the woman standing next to them. Their eyes seemed to carry the weight of several times the sadness, and Hannah knew instinctively that they were Summer's family.

Hannah went over to offer condolences, and introduced herself as Hannah Walter, that she'd met Summer at a Poetry Night and were friends. They seemed surprised, and the old woman held Hannah's hands. With her slightly raspy voice, she spoke.

"So you're Ms. Hannah Walter. I've heard many things from Summer."

"You did?"

"After Summer moved to Riverside, she felt a lot of loneliness. She's rather sensitive and couldn't easily find people who shared her heart, but everytime we talked on the phone, she'd mention you, and we knew she'd found someone she could rely on and felt safe… to think this would happen…" She couldn't finish her words, bursting into tears. Hannah could do nothing but hold her hands tighter.

The young woman standing next to the old woman, with a foreign image, straight nose, and double lids, held tightly onto the old woman's shoulders, and patted her. She was as tall as Clint, thin, and somewhat slender. The woman who resembled a fashion model introduced herself as Naomi Wu, Summer's younger sister. She also shook her hand, and the old man next to her introduced himself as Kyoo-In Wu. He also shook Hannah's hand without a word.

After a while, everyone sat in their seats, and the pastor began the funeral. Summer's mother seemed to want Hannah to sit with her, so Hannah and Clint sat to the mother's right, and Naomi and Kyoo-In sat to her left.

Throughout the funeral, Hannah felt the weak shaking of her hands, and felt her sadness wholeheartedly, as she heard quiet sobs of a mother. Hannah began to feel teary as well. She knew only too well, the feelings of those who'd lost someone. In the past, when her parents suddenly passed away from the car accident, Hannah felt as if she was locked in a tunnel, with no lights shining through. She remembered the time when she couldn't take a single step. She knew then that the most difficult and wretched memories etched themselves to the mind, and lasted the longest. Hannah had been able to let go of that sadness due to love, but Summer's parents couldn't do so! There was an old saying, that if one lost a child, they buried the child in the sky. Hannah understood the saying to mean that a parent must live their lives, always aware and in despair of their lost child. How could Hannah ever know how Summer's parents were feeling?

The casket lowered into the ground, and everyone threw in a red rose. Hannah finally realized it was time to accept the devastating truth: she'd never see her again. She no longer existed in this world. Considering the uncertainties behind just how and why she's died, although she was now buried in earth, those questions still lingered, completely open to the world.

Mr. Kyoo-In Wu hadn't dropped a single tear until that point, but as he saw the soil slowly being added on top of the grave, he could no longer hold himself in check, as he began to wailed. No one around him said a single word as they witnessed the evidence of sadness and pain with level so deep, it was nearly impossible to comprehend. Even for Hannah, Summer was like a sister, and a friend. The mile back after burying her felt much longer than before. It felt like walking on frozen earth, bleak and lonely austere of a walk. Filled with intense grief, she realized that flower tunnel could feel like a thorny Sweet Hallow, once more.

Soon returning home, Hannah walked into the study, and rolled herself into a ball in a chair, thinking of nothing, and closing her eyes. Clint came in a few minutes later, and put his hands on her shoulders. He said nothing. Then he took her hand and led her to the bedroom. He sat her down on the bed, and brought a warm tea, handing the cup to her. Clint then held her tightly. The two sat there, wordless, carelessly flowing like the river within time.

Clint went to work the next day as usual. When Hannah woke up and went to the kitchen, she found traces left by Clint on the dining room table. Being able to see traces showed existence. As she thought such things, she stared at the cheese spread, bagel crumbs, the red light on the coffeemaker, and the mug with leftover coffee, mind completely blank. She finished washing the dishes and brought a cup of black coffee into the study, sitting down on the chair and turning the computer on. The bright sunlight that had opened Hannah's day, and Beethoven she'd enjoyed was silent that morning.

The world had changed much the past few days. As she had trouble adjusting to a different morning, Hannah set her coffee mug down and paced around the room, before picking it back up and walking out to the kitchen. She drank her coffee and ate a bagel with strawberry cheese spread. The softness of the cheese spread, and the delicateness of the texture of the bread mixed in her mouth feeling almost symbolic, as if it were two peoples' way of mingling and feeling ecstasy. When thinking about it, Hannah was able to remember that the pleasure of eating was one of life's happiness.

As Hannah thought this or that, she pushed away the darkness of the room, and wiped away the dust on the turn table. She began to think that even dust shouldn't be treated lightly. She suddenly remembered the saying that when one died, they became dust.

But she thought that Summer would become a butterfly, rather than dust. As she flew around the world, she'd see much more and hear more, becoming wings of hope for those in despair, and melting into the hearts of tranquil and innocent children, running in the field, fluttering and dancing, laughing with children.

It was only a brief, fleeting thought, as the doorbell rang. It was the postman. He handed Hannah an envelope and asked for a signature. It was from Simon & Roadman Law Firm, and it was addressed to Hannah Walter. She signed it and thanked him. She locked the door and sat down on the sofa in the living room, before opening the envelope. There was a letter. It was from Mr. Simon, and explained that Hannah Walter was to inherit according to a Summer Wu's will. It directed her to come by the law firm by October 21, at 10:00 AM, to Simon & Roadman Law Firm on Taylor road. When Clint came home, she showed the letter to him, and told him that she had to go take care of this. He tilted his head, saying that it was strange and made no sense, since Hannah wasn't Summer's parent, nor sister; yet she was to inherit.

Hannah decided to go anyway. That morning, Hannah wore a black suit which were a few years old, a blouse with cloudy prints on a sky blue background, with blue silk scarf on her neck, and locked the door, before walking out to the driveway where her car was. As she hadn't left the house recently due to being sick, she felt the chilly temperature as she arrived at the fourth floor of the red building on Taylor Street, Simon & Roadman Law Firm. She parked her car at nearby parking lot and walked through the front door. A thin and courteous woman sitting in the entrance asked for her name and took her to the lawyer.

Mr. Simon's room on the fourth floor was surrounded by large windows. From the window, she could make out Richmond Island and Summer Lake Road. There were bookcases to the left and right of the room. Each of the bookcases were filled with law books, and golf club leaned on the bottom.

He was a cleanly shaven, sharp-looking man in his late fifties.

"Welcome, Ms. Walter."

"Hello, Mr. Simon."

"I am the attorney in charge of executing Ms. Summer Wu's will, and wanted to let you know that you are one of those inheriting under the will. She warned me that she would like your inheritance to be taken care of differently. So let's go." So they went to the nearby bank. After being taken to the vault of the bank, Hannah was still very much confused. Mr. Simon turned around and looked at Hannah in the vault.

"I believe you already have the key." Hannah's eyes widened. She had the key. She didn't know if this was the right key, but it was a key Summer had given her. Hannah quickly opened the purse and retrieved her key. Mr. Simon took the key and opened one of the boxes. He took the box out, and handed her a small box. Within the box was a traditional Chinese man's clothing, which was tattered and ripped. It was wrapping something, and when she opened it, was found out to be old tattered group of papers, tied together. When she opened the first page, she found an old photograph, and the paper had Summer's handwriting on it. Hannah took the items and left the bank with Mr. Simon. They returned to the law firm building, where she signed to confirm receipt of the items, and Hannah returned home. As soon as she returned home, she carefully untied the knot on the papers. Some were written in Chinese, and some were written in broken English. The first page was in Summer's writing, which simply said, "My Grandma, Sel Lin Chao's story."

Eleven

Early December, 1937, Zhenjiang

Father is still ill. Thankfully, Ha Lin and Qu Lin are maintaining the household by taking care of work at the fish market, but with the news of Shanghai being invaded by the Japanese Imperial Army, more people began to pack up and leave, so we were getting less customers by the day.

Last November, father fell and hurt himself severely as he was bringing in a cart of fish to sell, and could no longer work, those days becoming longer and longer as he failed to get up. These days, father had trouble getting up from bed in the morning, merely groaning in pain. The situation was becoming dire. Ha Lin has since gave up on his decision to go to university, and became the ad hoc family leader, maintaining the family fish market after graduating from high school. Qu Lin stopped by after school to help out, and then returned home in the evenings.

Yul Lin and I would take care of our father once we came home, and prepared food and finished any leftover house work. At first, father ate little bit of food, but these days, he's having trouble, not even glancing at the porridge. He slept most of the day and spent the day in bed, moving only to get to the toilet. He would lean all of his weight on a cane and take himself there, refusing any help to get to the toilet, even when in such pain.

As always, Ha Lin and Qu Lin returned home after a hard day at work, and worried after seeing father's state. Ha Lin finally told Qu Lin and me,

"Father's condition is worse than we expected. There's nothing we can do here… Most of the town medics have already fled, so no one can help us."

Qu Lin then replied, "Sel Lin and I will go to Nanjing."

I became curious as to whether uncle would still be at Nanjing. Since train from Shanghai didn't come these days, we would have to walk to Nanjing. I couldn't help but wonder whether Nanjing would be as empty as Zhenjiang, as people may have all left the city.

After mother passed away, my family didn't go to Nanjing as often anymore. I had some vague memory of Nanjing from when I was seven, but since I hadn't gone after that, I began to worry about Uncle's store being there. Big and small rooms, endless entertainment and things to see, and the aroma of boiling herbs; I decided to bet the success of this trip on Qu Lin, my second brother, two years older than I am.

"Mr. Wong came to the store today, and told me Shanghai fell to the Japanese imperialists." Ha Lin said, worry in his eyes as he looked at us.

Yul Lin held my shoulders as she hid her face behind my back. I could feel her warm but shaky breath. Leaving father in the hands of the 11 year old Yul Lin was not a comforting thought, but father's health was worsening by the day.

As our uncle didn't have children, he always welcomed us to his home, and the prospect of seeing him again was exciting, but I also couldn't shake the concerns that followed, like our ability to get there and whether he was still in the business of selling medicine there. But it wasn't as if we could just do nothing either.

Next morning, Qu Lin and I packed some fish which had been pickled and fried, as well as some rice, packed tightly, and began to make our way to Nanjing. We would have taken a train or a car before, but there were no cars, and trains didn't run anymore. We followed along the Yangtze River, walking on unpacked gravel road and kicking up dust on the dirt road, with holes here and there. I gasped nearly running to catch up to the faster pace of Qu Lin. Surprisingly, we weren't the only ones walking. Sometimes a cart with items tightly secured, or people sitting on such carts would pass us by. We tried to catch one, but they didn't seem to hear us; they were too busy escaping from the imminent attack by the Japanese. Many of the other carts had people hanging from them, desperate not to fall off and staring only ahead. It wasn't easy to find any kind of a car or cart that we could ask to get on.

I don't know how long we had walked. We finally sat down where the river's width widened, and rested while we had our lunch. As I'd never walked this long, I took my shoes off to rub at my swollen feet; there were birds flying above the river, free; as the river surrounded the mountains like a folding screen, filled carts continued to move away.

"Qu Lin, do you think we'll be able to meet uncle when we get to Nanjing?"

"I don't know… we won't know until we get there."

"Do you remember Nanjing?"

"Yes."

"How was Nanjing?"

"There is still a long way to go. Get ready."

Qu Lin didn't answer me and picked himself back up, but he never was very talkative. After we finished lunch, we began our walk again. I wanted to rest a little longer, but we still had a long way to go.

The Sun set before we knew it, and in the sky was a half moon and stars. The Big Dipper shone brightly. Moonlight in the cold winter looked clean and cold. Suddenly, Qu Lin grabbed my arm and whispered, "Down! Hide next to me!" I quickly threw myself flat next to him. Thanks to the reeds by the river, we could hide in safety.

Soon, military trucks began to pass by. The loud noise of the engine and the voices of men who spoke in a language I did not understand. As I felt the shaking ground beneath, I was afraid of them hearing my heart beating loudly against my chest from fear. I couldn't even breathe deeply, fearing condensation leaking from my lips. I don't know how long we waited. As my body felt completely frozen and we heard nothing, Qu Lin took his hand off of my back, and got up slightly to look around the reeds. He then gave a sigh and helped me up. I stood up, rubbing my arm.

As we continued our walk, we began to look for places to hide. We don't know how much longer we walked. From a distance, the sound of household goods shaking sounded similar to gong, ringing the quiet night. After the sound of wheels could be heard, a cart holding many household goods could be seen, shining under the moonlight. Qu Lin seemed to stare at the cart, before he walked to the front of it, and the cart stopped. The owner saw the two of us, and stopped suddenly, surprised.

"Please help us," said Qu Lin. I also followed suit, bowing. He agreed reluctantly, and told us to sit with his wife and children. We said a simple hi, before getting on.

"Where are you going?" asked the man.

"We're on our way to Nanjing," Qu Lin replied.

"Nanjing?" the man asked, clearly startled.

"Yes."

"Isn't Nanjing dangerous?"

"Is it? Then where are you all going?"

"I am coming from Shanghai. I was in another area because of work…"

"We left Shanghai after we heard the news of the Japanese army attacking Shanghai. We only took what we thought we needed… that was only a couple of days ago…" as his wife finished, the man nodded.

"Shanghai is no longer safe," said the man. "The Japanese have taken Shanghai, and are committing theft, murder, and rape. We have to go far away. It seems like you are young students, so let me advise you to leave Nanjing as soon as you need to do what you need to do. They say it's Nanjing next."

"Unfortunately, that's very difficult," replied Qu Lin. "Our father is sick, and we have to get medicine from Nanjing. Then we must return to Zhenjiang." I nodded at his words.

We went for a while in the cart on the night road up north. Soon, the cart stopped and we got off.

"Follow this road to go into Nanjing. Don't take the wide roads; go into the alleyway. I don't know how many people are left, so be careful. I wish you luck." And the family left for Beijing. As we saw his cart slowly move disappear into the darkness, the wheels making clunking noises, we followed the narrow alleyway into Nanjing.

It wasn't until nearly early morning that we managed to reach the entrance of the wall gates of Nanjing, where our uncle used to live.

The gray darkness, and the eerie silence swallowed up any remaining memories of my childhood, and Nanjing huddled in the middle of this depressing darkness. I saw many refugees. Some were shaking, and some stared at the sky, their eyes seemingly unfocused. Some people were completely bloody, wriggling in pain and gasping for their final breath, like caught fish lying on a bench, and those who were alive were crying in pain. Due to the Japanese bombardment, everything was burning and destroyed around the walls of Nanjing. We could hear the sound of shells and military boots, and the occasional flash lit up the night sky and showed us a glimpse of dark alleyway.

We were lost for while before finding a small marketplace located on the southern entrance, overlooking the city wall. The corpses littered the place, and children covered in dust and filth sat by the broken wall, shivering, shaking, and begging people for food. Qu Lin first found the small park located on the Southern entrance facing the Nanjing Castle Wall. As I stared at the park, the memories of when I was very young began to come back. When the parents and other adults conversed among themselves, we would go to the park and play with the other kids. Of course, the park was now nothing but a ruin, filled with corpses missing legs and arms. With the smell of waste and rotting flesh suffocating the air, I barely held in nausea as I walked closer to my brother.

Eventually, we found our uncle's pharmacy, as we hid from the view of people, and we couldn't hide the surprise at how different the place had become. The front door was long gone, and the bags of herbs and medicine that used to hang on the ceiling, and those that used to fill the walls were nowhere to be, and the big grandfather clock that was taller than father, or the long bench we used to sit on, while we watched people come and go. The large pharmacy was completely empty, with the exception of a half-burnt painting on the wall, wavering against the chilly winter wind. I was speechless. Qu Lin called for uncle, but no one replied. We quietly made our way to a small side door located behind the store. Behind the side door, in front of our eyes, was a half-sloping main house. The place where a beautiful garden used to be was barely recognizable, maintaining nothing but a fraction of what it used to be. After looking around, we came back out. Qu Lin seemed to be in thought, however, as he returned. He closed the side door behind me. I walked to a corner of the store with a bookcase, where a few herbal books still remained.

When mother was still alive, I used to play hide and seek with my brothers. I'd remembered dropping books by mistake, and witnessing the uncle coming out of the back to clean the mess on the floor. It was a plain bookcase, but it'd opened into something, like something mysterious. It'd opened to a secret room. I was simply too young to remember, yet Qu Lin had. It wasn't visible to the outside and was located far in the right corner of the main house, underground. When uncle's pharmacy was still successful, it was a location to store herbs and was known only to family.

Qu Lin pushed the bookcase away to reveal a small secret door and opened it. It was pitch dark and quiet inside. Qu Lin quietly whispered,

"Uncle?"

At first, we heard nothing. Then, my eyes got used to the dark, and I was able to see movement; I quickly hid behind my brother, shivering. Someone lit a candle, and there were my uncle and aunt, with much more wrinkles than I remembered.

"Qu Lin? And... you're... Sel Lin? How did you..." As I heard Uncle's shaking voice, I sighed with relief.

He stood up, only to hold our hands and telling us to have a seat, before closing off the secret room again.

Bags of herbs hung on one side of the wall, and aunt was lying on a small bed on the opposite side of the wall. There were a few cooking tools and materials on another corner, and a stove.

"As you're becoming older, Qu Lin, you're starting to look more and more like my sister."

"Is living here difficult for you at all, uncle?"

"We can handle the difficulties. No one but your family knows the location of this room. Of course, when we have to prepare food or go to the outhouse, it can be problematic. Nanjing simply is no longer safe," and uncle continued, "it's very late tonight... or is it too early...? Sleep tonight and we'll take care of whatever we need, tomorrow."

We all lied down in the small room next to each other, and I fell asleep as soon as I lied down.

Due to sickness, aunt had been unable to leave the bed for several days now. I helped uncle wash up aunt, and after talking with Qu Lin, uncle began to prepare herbs and medicine for us to take. We talked the whole day, and before we left for home early morning next day, uncle said,

"When you return, be careful and use mountain roads or those where people do not frequent. Sel Lin, you should change into my clothes. I hear that the Japanese cut up any woman down with a sword. Your hair is much too long as well, and we should cut it. If you're to get home safely, it'll be better to look like a boy.''

I changed into a man's shirt and pants. Uncle cut my hair, and as I watched my long locks of hair fall to the ground, I couldn't help but tear up. But I didn't cry. As uncle handed me bandage, he said,

''Make sure to wrap this around your chest,'' and left the room with Qu Lin briefly while I changed; when I opened the door, they reentered.

Uncle said,

''There are two roads outside of Nanjing. Just follow the road to the East. Once you go about 60 km, there will be three-way split fork. Take the one at the right. It'll be dark by then, so if the road gets wider, check the road briefly with the catchlight and turn it off immediately. If someone sees the light, you won't be safe anymore.''

Next early morning, before the Sun was up, uncle packed a steamed bread and oolong tea in a bag with leather straps along with father's medicine, and tied the bag to my brother's back. I said my goodbye to my aunt before I left the darkened room, wearing a warm jacket filled with cotton thanks to uncle. Her heavy eyes were filled with tears as she silently cried. I wiped her tears off with the sleeve, and after uncle left first, making sure no one was about, we left the secret room as well. The cold air of the early morning felt like a slap. We quietly said our goodbyes, as we began walking toward Zhenjiang, with Nanjing behind us. As we came out of the alleyway, I tried to not step on any corpses. I wondered how long we'd walked, since we left those walls behind? The sun began to rise over the horizon. We'd walked more after meeting the two-way fork in the road, but since our legs were sore and because we hadn't eaten breakfast, we decided to rest. We hid in the shade not very visible to the road, and took care of our rather late breakfast with a bread and oolong tea, taking a brief break. My feet were swollen from the tens of miles of walking done in the past couple of days, yet I wanted to return quickly to brew the medicine for father. Resting a little bit cooled our bodies down, making us feel cold, so we got back up and continued our way. The road taken with the rather reserved Qu Lin was boring and tedious, yet it wasn't the time to think about such things. Nanjing's fallen walls looked similar to that of a giant dragon, gagged. A dragon immobilized by the gag, unable to move, even a step, that anyone who saw it might feel just as bitter about it.

After walking silently for a while, my brother turned around and opened his mouth.

"Let's find that three-way fork before it gets dark. That way we won't have to light anything up until we get home, since weren't we able to go to Nanjing without light?"

"Yes, Qu Lin. We can do it. Let's do our best."

To the side of us was a knoll and to the left, was the Yangtze River, flowing quietly. As we continued down the ridge of the mountain, we stared at the Sun which had risen up past the river and shone a light on the endless amount of corpses on the riverside, which made me shudder. My heart was shrinking under the cold winter sunlight.

Twelve

Nanjing, December, 1937

Since leaving uncle's house, the Sun had set to the West, and whatever warmth and life that had shined over the waters of the River had gone, leaving only the cold exhausted air. Suddenly, the sound of gunfire rang out over the orange waters of the river. The following machine gun sound felt like thunder, splitting the air and ripping the sky apart. Qu Lin and I both were caught completely unaware. I froze on the spot, but Qu Lin quickly snatched my wrist and pulled me away from the road, hiding behind a steep slope. Then he peered up slightly to look toward the sound. I hid closely behind my brother, barely peeking at all. At the end of the sound were tens of people with their hands and feet tied, standing in a line by the riverbed. On the opposite side must have been Japanese soldiers, as they held submachine guns, in a ready position.

There were many people, already dead, covered in blood. Unable to do anything, I hid there, my body visibly shivering, my mouth agape, and my brother's big eyes were also focused on the scene below. He quietly helped me up, while he held my shaking hands, and whispered into my ear.

"Sel Lin, we can't be here. We need to run away before they find us here. Do you understand?"

Unsure of my ability to say anything, I nodded, gulping down air. He got up and waited for me to get up. As I tried to get up, I slipped on my weight and stumbled, and the metal water bottle that was on my back made a loud noise as it hit a rock and rolled away onto the other side. One of the men turned his head toward us. My brother pushed me down, and rolled down the hill down to where I'd stumbled down to. He quickly whispered,

"If he saw us, he'll start looking for us. I don't know if they saw you, but I think they saw me. One of us has to live and bring the medicine home. Let the family know what happened, tell them like Shanghai, Nanjing isn't safe anymore, and help them get out. Okay?"

I shook my head at Qu Lin. I replied,

"What are you saying!? Let's go together! I can't do this alone! I don't know where to go! We have to live or die together!"

"Be rational, and remember what uncle said. Those dead people were wearing civilian clothing. They're not POWs, they're people like you and me. If we get caught, we'll both die for sure. You trust me and you have to get to Zhenjiang safely. Please."

He gave me a few reassuring claps on my back, and soon after, we heard steps, of movement through the field of reeds. My breath got caught in my throat. Soon, we could see beams of light above us. We froze up like a rock. However, Qu Lin tied up the medicinal herb bag on me, and whispered,

"I'm going first, so hide until you hear absolute silence, and then walk away. If we're both alive, I'll see you at the three-way fork road," and began to walk away, jumping over the slope and going down once more. Soon, the beams, hearing my brother, began to shine on his direction instead, and I rolled my body up as small as possible underneath. I didn't know how long it had been, but I no longer see any light, and instead heard the sound of guns. I desperately hoped from my brother's safety, but couldn't help but be filled with despair. My legs were stiff and cramped, but fearing that there could be Japanese soldiers remaining, I couldn't move a step. Soon, the beams of light returned to the slope where I was hiding, and I froze, not even breathing properly. Soon, the light went back up the slope, and I could hear them say something amongst themselves, before the gunfire began again, and with the sound of moving truck, their sound eventually faded away. At first, I couldn't properly get up, and merely could crawl down the slope, flattening my body to the ground as much as I could. After a while, when there was no sound but the sound of the water, I barely managed to pull myself up, and saw no one. I couldn't measure how long I'd stayed there, but I hoped dearly that my brother would survive and come back, as I continued my way. I don't know how long I walked, shivering, alone, on a pitch dark night. I didn't even know if it were the right road, but all I could think of was returning home, and that made me continue. I could feel that the road widen rather rapidly. Suddenly, a light shone on my back. In front of me was the three-way fork that my brother told me before, but someone shouted in a foreign language from behind me, and I slowly turned around. Two soldiers got out of the truck and held their guns pointed toward me. I slowly raised my hand. They were Japanese.

With their rifle, they pointed it to the truck. I slowly made my way to the truck and right before getting on, threw the backpack on the side by the river. If there was any chance of my brother living and making it there, he needed to take the medicine home.

The soldiers suddenly yelled and pointed their rifles at me, and I raised my hand once more.

The soldier yelled out something in a language I did not understand. As I stood there awkwardly, another soldier said in Chinese.

"Get on the truck!"

Upon hearing it, I hurried up the truck the soldier pointed to.

One tried to get off of the truck to find my bag, but the truck began to move, and they sat down, their rifles never moving away from me.

I looked around carefully. There were about twenty men and women all quivering in fear. As if worried that someone may jump off of the truck, they held the guns pointed at us at all times. The truck took the leftmost fork from the three-way fork, and began to speed up. It made another left turn, and I could tell I was getting further away from my home again. Most of them wore civilian clothing, quivering without a word, feeling cold, and curled up next to each other. I also lowered my head as I heard the sniffles of the girl next to me. Even with uncle's warnings, we were still found by the Japanese. Depression came over me. The thought of never seeing Yul Lin, Ha Lin, or father again saddened me even more. But it wasn't as if being sad would change my destiny... I hoped they would be safe. I begged to my ancestors and to god.

Soon, we arrived back at Nanjing, where I'd left early in the morning . The truck stopped in front of a broken down storage facility, and the Japanese soldiers ordered everyone off, and had all of us stand in a line. I could smell blood from the Yangtze River flowing in front of the building.

The soldiers began to tie our arms behind our back. A mid-age woman begged for her child's life, but the soldier slammed her head with the rifle. Blood began to drip from her head, and she fell on her face.

Soon, the front door of the truck opened, and a man with sharp eyes and a pistol on his side got out of the car as he stared at us. To be exact, he seemed to be looking at me. But I didn't avoid his stare. Maybe it was because I realized that I could become like the fallen woman, that this would be the last thing I saw.

He walked toward me. I stood up even straighter, trying to convey confidence. Soon, he stood in front of me, and everyone quieted down. He then stared at my eyes as he opened his lips and said something to the soldiers, then took my wrist roughly. He then sat me down in the front seat of the truck. The other three soldiers all pushed the civilians with their rifles. The rest of the people were soon forced to walk down to the riverside, and I sat on the truck with the man. Suddenly, he rushed forward, laid me down on the seat, then opened his pants. I closed my eyes tightly. Then he quietly said in Chinese,

"I will hide you, so do as I say," He then redid the knots in his pants, and I just lied there.

"Follow the Quinwe River to Fuzimiao near Purple Mountain. Our soldiers monitor the area, but it's been bombed and the area is completely demolished. It's of no use to anyone. The only thing you will find will be pieces of statues strewn about on the yard. Building itself is nothing but ash. Look to the left of the building, and you'll find a half collapsed wall adjacent to the right side of the main sanctum. There is a door at the opposite side of the collapsed wall. It will look like part of a wall, but it isn't. Press the right edge of the wall and walk down into the underground. There is a hidden location underneath the stairs. Stay there and don't come out. No matter what loud sound you hear, do not look out or come out."

He said and opened the truck door to look around. I don't have any reason to trust of what he said but there was not much of choices that I made.

He said to me hurry up and shots two times at the ground where I stood near by.

I hid in the dark once more, without being able to see the people I'd been with.

I moved up to bank of the Quinwe river without rest, and was covered in dirt and blood as I tripped over endless amount of corpses. I couldn't smell a thing, nor could I feel anything. I just had to get away from this dangerous place. There were so many dead naked women by the riverside. Some of them had wooden sticks on their lower parts and were strewn away on the river bank, and the corpses of children looked like little balls. If I thought I heard any sound of a truck, I'd hide amongst the corpses, and only when the truck passed by completely, then I'd get back up and continue. It didn't feel as if I were alive. It felt like a nightmare. Just a few days ago, I was living in Zhenjiang as a normal person. And today, I nearly died twice, and now, I was walking on dead bodies of people, knee deep in blood, as my legs kept getting buried in the mud and blood.

I walked all night and managed to get into the Fuzimiao sanctum right before dawn. There were at least six Japanese soldiers in front, and I quietly treaded to the back, before I entered. I was so afraid of them possibly smelling the blood on my body, but thankfully, it seemed that they hadn't smelled me.

As the Japanese officer told me earlier, Fuzimiao sanctum seemed unrecognizable due to the bombardment. At the top of the stairs where Confucius' statute would be, was bits and pieces of him, just barely maintaining some resemblance of shape. Behind the main sanctum, burnt fragments of the building stood as skeleton; no one would possibly believe that this place was a birthplace of China's most learned, or that it was a place holding the soul of China for thousands of years. To the left, the side buildings seemed to hold the memories of the history's most darkest moment, with its burn marks. Far away, it felt as if the Sunset behind Purple Mountain was taking its last breath, bringing in the icy early evening.

I pushed the wall which was an opposite side of the collapsed wall as he had said. I nearly tripped and tumbled down the stairs a few times, but held onto the railings at the side to stable myself. I found it when I had subconsciously flailed about trying to grab onto something. As I reached the end, I could feel flat floor. There wasn't anything I could see or feel in the dark. I was too exhausted, and fell to a corner, and found I had no strength left after such a traumatic and full day. I looked around and saw small wooden boxes stacked on top of one another. There was a small gap above the boxes. It was a small opening connected with the rest of the world.

I looked around. There were small wooden boxes stacked on top of one another and a small jar in one corner. There is a small window was opened to the world.

The room was isolated from the rest of world, accepting only a single ray of early morning light, and frozen in time. On one side were clothes that someone may have worn until recently. It was a man's clothing. I took off my bodied clothes and put on the slightly softer shirt. The room's only window, which was very small was quite high up, that it required at least five boxes to be stacked on top of one another see the outside. The window was attached to the flat side of the stairs that went up to the main sanctum. It was difficult to see from the outside, but the outside was visible from the inside. All of the buildings as skeleton had silently watched the countless amount of people get killed that night, facing the wall, and shading their bodies from the light.

I wonder how long it had been since then? I fell asleep, sitting underneath the window, curled up underneath, probably from exhaustion. When I woke up, the Sun was high up in the sky. I wanted to go to the bathroom, and I was hungry. I realized I hadn't eaten anything since breakfast yesterday, when I had a piece of bread and some tea for late breakfast with Qu Lin. I got up from my spot. My entire body was sore and stiff. I also could smell the stink off of my body. Although I had changed out of my clothes yesterday, I hadn't been able to wash up. I wanted to look around, but as I got up, moving around created a fear inside me. I remembered the soldiers who had been standing there on a watch.

But the well-rested body wanted food and to take care of bodily urges. Inevitably, I blocked off the small window by stacking wooden boxes, one by one. In the darkened room, I slowly moved about, using my hands to feel around the area. When I walked further down, I saw a small side door, and when I opened it, I saw lavatory to the back. There was a bamboo watercourse of sort where water could flow in from the mountain to the underground of the building. Perhaps if one saw from the outside, no one could see anything. Someone had engineered the area so the lavatory was inside the building, behind everything, and had allowed use of water from the inside through the bamboo water channel. Perhaps someone had lived underground. Although I was still starving, just the ability to use the lavatory was enough for now. Then I returned to the room and hid. I hid near the windows again. I had to wait until that man appeared again. Soon enough, the sun began to set, filling the room in orange, and I stared at the slow decrease of light in the room. Whether the person decided to kill me or keep me alive would be something to be decided then, and I was still thankful for his telling me of this place.

As I began to get lost in thought, I heard someone walk toward the main sanctum, and come inside. I hid my body even further, hiding my body in the darkness, hoping it wouldn't be a Japanese soldier. But the person that'd appeared was him. He came into the door and blocked the moonlight shining into the window completely. He then turned the lamp on and began to talk in Chinese.

"You've arrived. Congratulations on surviving."

I bowed down to him.

"Thank you for saving me."

"Do you think I saved you?" He smirked.

I raised my head and looked at him properly.

"Well, since I was kept alive thanks to it, I needed to express my thanks."

He seemed to be satisfied by the answer, as he nodded.

"Ha ha ha! Well, if you say so."

"How did you know about this place?" I asked,

"Ah… you weren't a boy, but a girl. Why are you wearing a man's clothing? Your hair is also short."

"I heard the Japanese military raped any women or girls… if I were man, I would be safer…"

"Did you choose to dress up like this?"

"Yes," I answered right away. This man was still a Japanese soldier. I didn't want to alert him to the existence of my aunt or uncle.

"Well, aren't you special." Then he went to a corner and brought something to me.

"It's raw rice. You probably didn't have anything to eat until now. Eat."

I accepted the raw rice and quickly chewed on it. I'd never thought anything was as delicious as this. It tasted as sweet as honey. Although I hadn't let go of all of my inhibitions around him, I didn't have the luxury to refuse the food he'd offered me.

He said, "I've received the order to kill any Chinese we see," from the Imperial government.

"You are a lucky child!" he exclaimed, "I could have killed you. Everyone you'd been with in the truck are all dead, and were thrown away on the riverside. You must think of meeting me as your luckiest event in life." I nodded and once again gave my appreciation. He brought the lamp closer to my face and carefully examined my face.

"While we completely conquer Nanjing, and the Imperial government sets up a provincial government here, I will visit this place once a week. This place used to be Nanking University. As soon as the war occurred, they fled to Chongqing. They probably left some food you could eat. If you walk towards the back, you'll find the lavatory that were used by those who had studied here. There is even a place where you'll find water. Use water in the afternoon. Soldiers are sensitive to sound at night. If you want to leave, leave. But know that if you do, I can no longer protect you. Whether you die from hunger, whether the soldiers rape you, or whether they shoot and kill you."

I couldn't answer back easily. I was simply too worried about my family in Zhenjiang. I wondered about whether Qu Lin was alive and Ha Lin, Yul Lin, and father's states. Not knowing what pain or torture they may be facing, I wondered whether I could simply stay safe here, alone. He didn't seem to care about my answer though, however.

"Sleep. I will be returning to base," with that, he got up. As he left, I could hear him close the door and lock it. I realized nowhere in Nanjing was safe. I turned the lamp off. I laid out the various clothes on the slightly thick straw mat and lied down. Maybe it was because I had slept all day; I couldn't sleep that night. My current situation simply was too surreal and worrisome, just as much as my family's whereabouts and safety. The fact that I could do nothing at that moment made me feel useless.

I fell asleep. In my dream, I slipped on endless amount of corpses surrounding the Yangtze River, completely soaked with their blood. The corpses were dead, yet their eyes captured every one of my movements. I tried to escape their eyes, but couldn't. They followed me until the end, with blood streaming down their eyes. I ran and ran, before tripping over another corpse, and hitting my head hard on the ground. In an instant, I was a corpse like them. Except for my eyes, I couldn't move a thing. Red rain fell from the sky, wetting my face. Once I realized, "I'm dead!" my eyes opened immediately, and I found my body soaked in cold sweat.

From nearby, I could hear the sound of rifles and shells explode, mixed with the screams and cries of people. It filled the room. I blocked my ear to the best I could, and slightly opened the window screen. Soon enough, the morning came, and only birds moved freely inside the sanctum. The tiny slicer of light barely lit the area inside.

The things I couldn't see last night began to show themselves under the bright sunlight. I looked around and went through the items in the room.

A desk, chair, and books filling a bookcase to one wall, rice, and clothes that students must have worn, neatly organized. I took the small gourd that had contained the sweet potatoes and walked to the lavatory, where I cleaned my body using the water provided, as a monk may have done at one point. The cold and clean water washed away the dirt and blood from my body. I even washed my face and hair, and threw away all of the water in the lavatory. Although my body was shivering from the cold, I couldn't possibly keep living with the blood of the dead on my body. I looked around as I ate another piece of the dried sweet potato. The room was filled with books. I took the book closest to me and began to read.

In one of Confucius' books, "A man of virtue gives goodness to others, but a man of pettiness takes of what he may receive." Was this the case... I thought.

What did China do so badly that Japan could punish it so. Aren't the Japanese the petty people? Since they had desired China... but why was China subject to the whims of such petty people, and receive this kind of a result?

My head began to hurt. For a rather diligent person like me, this isolated space felt like a prison. Although the man had said this was the safest place, my conclusion was that I couldn't believe him. I didn't know what he wanted, yet I couldn't come and go as I wished, and it frustrated me. I hoped I could bring them all here, but the fact that I couldn't even guarantee my own safety if I left here utterly frustrated me.

The sunlight of the winter afternoon piercing through Fuzimiao Sanctum was painful and cold as the end of a knife.

Thirteen

Nanjing, January, 1938

I think it's been a month since I've arrived here. Everyday, I look out the window, stacking the boxes and stepping on top. The thing I desired to see outside was the Moon. When I left and returned to Nanjing, it was a half moon, and since it had been a full moon at least once, I could sort of tell how long it had been. In this small room, I'd stayed hidden for a month. I'd promised myself that I'd return home one of these days. That if I saw something had gotten better, that I would return to Zhenjiang. But instead of getting better, the smell of corpses and blood only got stronger.

Every night, the air filled with the sound of Japanese soldiers shooting their guns at civilians, and people screaming. When that happened, I curled my body into a ball near the wall, and blocked my ears.

The man who'd said he'd come every week did not appear every week. When he did, he would give me some food, talk briefly, and left. He said he was called Yoshihiro Saito, a general born from the Japanese occupied Chosun. When Japan began occupation of Chosun, he was studying in Manchuria, and was now a first lieutenant for Japanese Imperial military. He knew more about China than I did. And he mocked China.

"China is now Japan's land, and will never be able to escape the claws of Japan. Mark my words, as the great Imperial Japan will use China as the stepping board to swallow up this continent, and will continue onto Europe. From the land to the sea, there will not be a single place left untouched.

His descriptions gave me chills down my back. The idea of the entire world being soaked with the rifles of Japan and blood made me shiver in fear. But Yoshihiro continued.

"The Chinese sought useless land and useless achievements... they were too busy fighting amongst themselves as soon as their government broke down. Their inability to read the flow of time has helped Japan. With Meiji restoration, improved and advanced Japanese Empire has come to enlighten and to provide a better future for you. There will always be friction when one enters another's land. But people will adjust and live accordingly or die."

I was filled with anger. They had cruelly killed and raped so many people, polluting the Yangtze River with the blood of the Chinese, yet they expected us to accept it!? But I held back. Although Yoshihiro had saved my life, he was still a Japanese soldier. He could have killed me immediately, or taken me to the riverbed and had another soldier kill me. So I never showed my anger or annoyance at him.

I asked him once,

"Why did you save me?"

He seemed to think before replying,

"It's not important. You don't need to know. Memorize hiragana properly." He said I had to learn Japanese in difficult times to save my life. He then brought a Japanese textbook, and told me to read, write, and repeat.

One time, he brought something that wasn't food. He said,

"This is called a camera, and it's from Germany. It's of an excellent quality."

"Where did you get it?"

"There isn't anything a first lieutenant of the Imperial Japanese military can't get."

Then he suggested we take a photograph.

"But… wouldn't taking photograph with a Chinese person be a problem for you?"

"Don't worry. No one will see it."

So we took a photo. In a room with just that one sliver of light coming in, we stood there, taking a photo.

And for a while, he didn't appear again.

I spent most of the time eating the food he brought, reading, and studying the Japanese textbook.

No matter how much time had passed, it couldn't alleviate the loneliness. My mind never wandered too far from Ha Lin, Qu Lin, or Yul Lin. Was father still okay? Is everyone still alive? Thoughts of them filled my head.

I've been having the same nightmare every night. The bodies of dead people by the riverside, and with them, I stare at the rainy sky. The smell of blood and rot stuffs the air. A dragon flies out of the Yangtze, crying. I wanted to yell at the dragon to take me with him, but from the mouth that I couldn't even breathe in air, nothing came out.

That night, I woke up abruptly from the same nightmare. I wasn't alone. The dark room was hot and steamy, filled with gasps and moans. Worried that someone may be hurt, I turned the light on. At the end of it were two men wrapped around each other. The bottom was someone I didn't know, and the one on top was Yoshihiro Saito. The man and I were both surprised at the same time, but Yoshihiro didn't seem very fazed. Unknowingly, I backed away, and before I knew it, I was outside.

The place I'd been hiding in for the past month was colder than a month before. I could see my breath as air came in and out. As I stood there dumbfounded, breathing, I felt the cold air slowly creeping around me, cooling me down. I began to pace. Surrounded by the cold winter night air, I tried my best to understand. How… it was man and a man… was such a thing possible? Then I remembered the man who I didn't know. He seemed to resemble me somehow. And at that moment, I was able to understand everything.

The small sky that I had stolen glances of in the past no longer was contained in any form; it seemed to look down on this crazy world with cold eyes. As I slowly walked down the sanctum stairs, I froze on the spot. There were two Japanese soldiers holding their rifles at me. I slowly backed up, but fell after tripping. One of the Japanese soldiers asked me

"What —— you doing? You were hiding here? —— friend? Chinese——? Right? Explain! Or we'll kill you!" Although I couldn't understand everything, I recognized some from the conversations I had with Yoshihiro.

I raised my hand and shook my head. They came closer and looked closer, then whistled with each other. The words that came out of their mouths next froze me.

"Breasts, female, female~!"

I had forgotten to wrap my chest with bandage.

"Eh… I thought I wouldn't even get to taste any woman because of that shit lieutenant~ lucky, lucky!"

I began to shiver. I knew what they were going to do. I remembered the lifeless bodies of numerous women. I yelled at them in the Japanese I knew.

"Let me live! Stop! Don't do it!" But they had already pinned me on the floor, and ripped my shirt and pants off. The stone floor on that January night was as cold as ice, and I felt a new dreadful pain for the first time in my life. I wanted to cry and scream, but I couldn't say anything due to the shock.

"Talk about luck! Virgin! I didn't know there were virgins left in Nanjing!" The man above me yelled, as he panted excitedly.

"Hey! Hurry up! I would have done it first if I knew she were virgin! Damn!" The man holding the gun said.

The first man soon finished and moved out, and took the gun from the other man. Then he did the same thing. I finally screamed, initial shock gone.

"Ah! You trash, get off! Stop! I'll kill you!"

But the soldier slapped me so hard, I nearly bit my tongue.

"Shut up, you dirty Chinese! Accepting the Japanese man is an honor! You stupid idiot!" And he also panted, never stopping.

I closed my eyes and waited for him to be done. Suddenly, he stopped, and I opened my eyes ever so slightly. His eyes were wide open, and through his chest was a sharp sword, shining under the moonlight. Soon, the sword fell out, and the soldier fell on my body. I pushed his body out and crawled out. When I looked up, the other soldier was quivering and had dropped his head. The man holding a long katana-like sword was Yoshihiro.

"I see… you decided to dirty my prize, Tanaka."

"Lie.. Lieutenant Saito! We… didn't know she was your woman!" The soldier barely made it out.

"But you did dirty it. How will you repay?" Saito's eyes were colder than anyone else's.

"I'm sorr——-!!!" The soldier never could finish talking. The sword plugged into the man's stomach, and he fell to the ground. Yoshihiro talked, without looking at me.

"Return. I'll take care of this." Then he dragged their bodies outside.

I couldn't think of anything for a long time, but could understand what had happened as I saw the two dead soldiers. However, my body didn't react properly, and when I could no longer feel anything on my fingers, I got up. I walked down the stairs. I put on pieces of fabric that used to be my clothes. The sharp wind came through my ripped skin. Blood dripped from the ends of my flesh. I dragged my leg as I quietly left the sanctum. The giant statue of Confucius looked down on me.

I looked up at the sky. It was a full moon, brightening up the sky. How long had I walked? I continued to limp down the riverside, filled with corpses. It wasn't a coincidence that I'd always felt like a dead person, not so different from them. I thought I was already dead. The dead under the moonlight looked like white pear flowers. It looked as if the moonlight was mourning those who had already long gone. I walked for a while before hearing someone run towards me. I looked back to find Yoshihiro. He told me to stop, but I continued. He was faster though, and grabbed at my arm. I hit the arm that touched me reflexively. But he didn't even blink.

"I understand what just happened to you, but you will die if you continue. You'll be raped until you're considered useless, and then you'll be killed. Be calm."

But I didn't want to return there, so I continued to limp away. Then I tripped over a corpse, and it must have been loud enough as searchlight began to shine in my direction, glancing over the many dead people as it passed. He took me down to the riverbed. And he hold me up to the top of riverbed when the light was gone. We followed the stairs down again. It was dark once more, and we sat there without a word. There was no light in this underground place, just darkness.

From then on, I lied there and slept for days without moving. Compared to before, my desire to live had significantly decreased. That nightmarish night had a full moon over the sky, which had lit their ugly faces, but tonight was dark.

Once I finally became aware, I took of my clothing to wash it. No matter how hard I rubbed at it, the blood refused to come off. Just like blood on a white field of snow, the blood on my white Chungsam only became a dark brown stain, and refused to go away. I put the clothing on top of a small wooden box, and when it dried, used a small wrapping cloth to wrap it up. I didn't want to show it to anyone nor see it myself. I couldn't throw it away, however, because it reminded me of my uncle's wrinkled hands. But would I ever be able to see them again? I felt like I had done something wrong. To my family that I'd been forced away, they could no longer expect me to be their little Sel Lin. I was barely breathing in a world and time, where I could no longer rely on anyone.

Yoshihiro came again. I didn't look at him properly. I didn't even know what to say to him. He asked,

"Is your body okay?"

I didn't answer him. But it seemed that he didn't really want me to answer him either.

"I couldn't come here due to the two soldiers I had taken care of."

I looked at him blankly, before opening my rather dry lips.

"What's the date today?"

"It's February 20th," he answered.

It's been nearly two months since I left my home. I still couldn't stop wondering whether father was okay, whether Qu Lin was able to return safely, and whether Ha Lin and Yul Lin were still doing well. But there were so many reasons why I couldn't go back or go out. Fear was no longer just an emotion; it was reality.

Due to my optimistic nature, depression wasn't able to affect me for too long, but the very real fear of someone taking my body and life kept me there.

My breasts seems to have gotten much larger recently. I also hadn't seen my face in a very long time. The girl with a lot of dreams, Sel Lin Chao. The round face taken after my mother, with tall nose, and the only one without the double lids on my eyes, and my rather plump features made me look very pretty in a dress, or so my father had said, so he'd always bought me qipao with large peony prints on them. Sometimes, I'd come home to find Yul Lin wearing my qipao and doing different poses. As I looked at her, I tried my best not to laugh. The qipao which came all the way down to her ankles looked like a giant sack on her, although it only came down to her calves. She was four years younger than me, but much taller. She was also very thin, and people often thought I was the younger child as a result. Sometimes boys would take a glance at me when I wore my qipao out, but those days were long gone, and I was no longer the same Sel Lin.

From then on, Yoshihiro no longer praised Imperial Japan. Whenever he brought Japan up, I'd start gagging. After doing so for several times, he stopped talking about Japan. I had an inkling that he continued to come here the about the same time, although he didn't show himself as often.

Yoshihiro was a paradox. He's a Japanese soldier, but he's not Japanese. He was brutal but kind to me. He loved a man rather than woman.

These days, I was having trouble with learning my mind. If more rational people who were understanding of their own emotions ruled the world, had they studied Confucius Mencius, and *The Four Books and Five Book of Confucianism,* perhaps Japanese soldiers would not use force to attack other countries and kill so many civilians… or so I thought.

I've not been able to eat anything recently either. After the rape, if I tried to eat, I'd end up throwing all of it up, remembering them. No matter how much I forced myself to eat, it didn't work. The nightmare I'd been seeing every night had a new scene now. In my dreams, not only could I not move, the soldiers would rape me every night, before I became a corpse, unable to move, and soaking completely in the blood of my own dead body.

I suffered sleep paralysis every morning, and when I'd finally come to, I'd be exhausted mentally and physically, as if my body were made of cotton soaked in water. My conversations with Yoshihiro decreased even more. He'd ask whether I had any difficulties, but I never answered him. No, I couldn't answer him. I'd seem to have forgotten all of the words I'd learned. The emotional and contemplative of me no longer existed. I simply lived day by day, getting closer to death by the Yangtze. Since I never went outside, the only thing I could do was open my ears to the darkness inside. Sometimes, I'd hear the crying sound of kids looking for their mothers, sound of people running, sound of army boots marching, and if not that, gunfire from far away. In the already dead city, there were no sounds of happiness.

One day, Yoshihiro appeared and said,

"Work here is nearly done. We plan to go to Manchuria. If you want, let's go together. I'll protect you to the best of my abilities."

But I shook my head. I didn't want to be any more of a burden to this man, and I wanted to end it here. I'm not his family. I had family somewhere else. Yul Lin and Ha Lin, and of course, Qu Lin... father. And even my uncle and aunt living in this city. I desperately hoped that they'd avoided the tornado of blood. I couldn't even think to escape to their home, worried I might bring them misfortune.

He tried to persuade me to no avail; he couldn't break my stubbornness. With a sigh, he returned. I thought that perhaps he'll never return here, yet he did, and continued to converse with me. Although he never had such a need to do so.

My siblings would sometimes freely debate about things that they were confused about or current events after coming back from school. When they did so, I was able to broaden my horizon on things I'd never thought of. Whenever Yul Lin asked "Why?" the second oldest, Qu Lin would always explain everything to her, and Ha Lin, the oldest, would organize everything, and I missed those days. These days, I thought about that a lot, and regretted that those days would never come back, which left a tightness in my chest.

One time, Ha Lin returned home very excited.

"Japan said Manchuria was the land of honey. Japan started this war and took Qindao, all to take Manchuria from us! That land is ours! We had to take it back under the Lausanne Treaty! They left the League of Nations so they could keep Manchuria! Only if the Kingdom was still strong! We wouldn't live like this!" Not knowing anything, I tried to placate him.

Qu Lin answered calmly,

"The monarch was rotting and weak. Old and rotting government is of no use to the people. We need a new government for all citizens, one that is powered by citizens."

Ha Lin replied, "Are you talking about communism...? Do you think it'd actually succeed?"

"Do you think the monarch succeeded?" Qu Lin would then retort, and they'd debate hotly for hours. Father would simply smile, happily stating, that China's future should be as hot and passionate as they were. Although all these things only existed in the past, in my own mind now...

Fourteen

Nanjing, March 1938

For the past few weeks, I hadn't been able to properly wash up. But recently, the stink was unbearably strong. There were corpses in every valley and forest, that the water flowing into the well smelled of only rotting flesh, that it was impossible to go near it. As the temperature continued its upward direction, the rotting only sped up.

Yoshihiro told me of his background life. When he lived in Chosun, his parents forced a marriage on him and gave birth to a daughter. He didn't love his wife, and left his wife after two years, soon obtaining the chance in a military academy. He didn't like talkative woman. I nodded, but I felt that he didn't just like talkative woman, just that he didn't like woman in general.

My body has been weird for a while. I was frequently dizzy and felt as if I would faint, and began to react strongly to smell. I often felt nauseous, and couldn't eat anything. I was also incredibly sleepy. I couldn't open my eyes, I was so tired. I didn't know what to do. So that whenever he'd brought something to eat, I wouldn't touch it at all, just turning around.

One day, he came, in a proper military suit. I realized our end had come. He handed me one piece of paper,

"Won't you come with me?" asked me once more.

I shook my head. His eyes were filled with sadness.

"Perhaps it's time to end our relationship here," and fixed his clothes and hat properly, before leaving sanctum. I looked at him going away, before reading the paper.

Meeting you here in China has been very helpful to me. I hadn't been able to sleep properly. I'd betrayed my country and swore allegiance to my enemy, and I always knew I'd never be able to raise my head properly toward my motherland. I have become the perfect traitor, handing to my enemy, lives of many people and the land. Like before, I will continue to take the orders of Imperial Japan. But I cannot take the things I've earned from Nanjing, especially when I consider you.

A moonlight shining at an angle, in this place, take four of the bricks out, and find a safe. It's my condolence to China and you. War is just war, and I have no special feelings toward Chinese or China, and I hope you'll understand it. It is still dangerous, so be careful.

3, 4, 23, 22

Yoshihiro Saito

After reading the paper, I couldn't hold in my anger. What did he mean, war is just war!? The acts they forced on us weren't what humans should have done! They treated us as animals, and committed endless killings! After all of that… to seek such easy penance, … my entire body shook in disbelief and anger.

Yes, he saved me. He killed the men who raped me, and didn't rape me. But before he met me… he killed so many people, Chinese, Koreans, and even others who were weak. He was going to keep killing. After reading his note, my anger toward the Japanese couldn't be controlled.

If Yoshihiro was correct, none of the Japanese soldiers probably don't have such strong feelings toward China. But does their feelings even matter?

I contemplated and agonized, before finally deciding. I didn't need his good will. I decided to leave everything here and return home. Whatever was in that safe was nothing but a burden.

The past month, whatever I ate, I'd regurgitate, and if I tried to eat, I had no appetite. My pants felt tighter, and I thought I'd felt fatter. It was strange. I hadn't eaten much at all last month. My arms were stick thin. But my stomach felt full. And then I remembered… last month, I didn't have my period. The first time I bled, a lady in my town took me to her house, where she gave me some bandages and diapers, and told me,

"You're now a woman. Don't worry. It happens every month, and it's your body telling you that you're now a woman."

Something was wrong with my body. But I couldn't find a doctor in this situation. So I decided that I needed to leave Nanjing. It was still very dangerous. Japanese soldiers still roamed around in Nanjing. A few people managed to come into the sanctum and talked about how the Japanese were now mass burying both dead and live people. These people hid into the sanctum at night, but by morning, I couldn't hear them. They weren't staying in one place for too long either. I was here for too long as well. I decided to set my goal as returning home alive. And I encouraged myself to live. I also had to fix whatever was wrong with my body. Before I went home, I wanted to erase whatever memory of Nanjing that was growing in my body.

I decided to leave Fuzimiao that night. I prepared some rice packed my uncle's clothes and a few pairs of clothing I could change into. I then left. I took the same side door and came back out.

As the darkness fell upon the night, I went up the rather steep hill behind the sanctum. Even in darkness, the large rocks seemed to cast a folding screen, standing with its head proudly out. I went up the lowest rock. Then I took a breath and looked around. The mountain seen after sunset seemed to show me my life. Lonely and stumbling in the unseeable darkness was me, Sel Lin. Spring evening's rock was wet and slippery.

Suddenly, I felt that I was falling into an endless abyss. I tried to grab at anything, even a grass nearby, but there was nothing but the air. I felt that I was being sucked into a maze. As I fell into the darkness, someone saw me and extended a hand. My body shook uncontrollably. As I continued down, my consciousness could not escape the vortex, and I felt my body fall apart into one, two, and three parts. At the end, I stopped right in front of a door.

I tried to open the door, but it wouldn't open, so I struggled. Someone came with a candle. His face became visible to me. I opened my eyes. I was lying down inside somewhere dark. The man made me drink water. He seemed to be the man who had extended his arm to me just moments earlier. I looked about and saw it wasn't a house nor the sanctum. I couldn't move a finger. My entire body felt like it'd rip. I teared up. It was so painful. I couldn't hear a thing he was saying, nor who he was. Then I must have lost consciousness.

A girl was crying sadly as she left my arms. I felt sad for her, so I tried to reach out to her, but she went away. It was a dream.

Fifteen

Nanjing, April 1938

The bright Sunlight shone over my feet. I looked up.

It felt like a cave or some sort of rock cavern. When I opened my eyes, someone was lying next to me. I tried to get up, but with a "ugh" groan, I couldn't say a thing nor move a thing. There was a boy under the age of one sleeping. Not knowing what's going on, I looked around the best I could. Then I heard someone walk in. I lowered my breath and tried to stay as still, and ever so slightly opened my eyes to look at the intruder. An unknown man brought in some firewood and came in. He looked in my direction and talked to himself,

"Still not awake… is she going to be all right…?" and came closer. He then put his hand on my forehead. I flinched involuntarily.

"Are you awake? Are you okay?!" He asked.

I tried to talk, but from my throat, only the sound "Ah," came out.

"I found you when I went outside. This is a rocky mountain behind the Fugician Tunnel. A lot of people escaped to Nanjing after Shanghai collapsed. I've been living here. I happened to luck out and found this cave, and have been living here since. It's pretty safe. Due to its hidden location deep in the forest and rocks, Japanese soldiers won't be able to spot it easily. Don't worry."

Then he said to me.

"You had heavy bleeding. I was very worried that you might not be able to make it."

"Ah..."

"Ah..., don't try to speak. You were very hurt. Perhaps you may have a bone or two broken." And he slowly helped me up. He gave me a porridge made with carrots, potatoes, and rabbit meat.

I wanted to thank him, but my throat refused to allow a voice. Afterwards, he told me to rest and helped me back down. I fell asleep once I was flat on my back. I was safe from pain then.

I don't know how long I lived in that cave. But I was finally able to speak again. He said he was traveling from Shanghai with his wife to the safety of Nanjing, but saw people leaving Nanjing as well. Realizing Nanjing wasn't safe, and got lost in the mountains, and found this place. Wife had been sick after giving birth to their son, but passed away last winter after heavy snow. His eyes were filled with tears.

I tried to console him, and he told me about the things he's endured.

"I used to work for the Kuomintang government in Shanghai. One day, I found a document while working. It said that the Kuomintang was receiving aid from the Japanese imperial government. But because I worked there and fed my family that way, I decided to quit and make a living as a farmer instead. But nothing is free in this world, you know. Imperial Japan invaded Shanghai, and except for my child, I lost everything." He said, tears flowing from his eyes.

"If I'd revealed that information and helped the communists, would my wife still be alive?"

I couldn't answer him. Would this one person's behavior be able to change history? I... don't know. Yoshihiro saved me but killed everyone else. Would my staying alive be enough to change history?

A few days after somewhat recovering, I decided to try again from Zhenjiang. I could walk better, and I heard the Japanese soldiers were going elsewhere. I thanked the man who saved my life. I thanked him and as I said goodbye, I told him that if we met again, it would be under a better, more comfortable circumstance. He told me to be careful on the road. He said to not use the commonly used roads, but to go via mountainous roads back. I said I would, and slowly got up. I slowly made my way down the mountain. My legs were quivering and shivering.

I walked and walked. And around early evening, I managed to return to the three-way fork that I'd arrived at so many months ago. Everything around it was rotting and burnt. This time though, no one stopped me. Of course, I'd nevertheless took caution, being careful to hide and be unseen. After walking without rest, I managed to return home before the sun rose, next day. I walked into the house.

"Yul Lin? Ha Lin? Father?"

The house was dark, and nothing could be heard. I yelled a bit louder, but no one answered. As I looked around, the house wasn't very different from when I had left. My body came down with a sudden chill, from feelings of fear and uncertainty. I entered the house, cleaned. Thankfully, the some of the dried fish hadn't rotted yet, so I ate them. I thought about taking the monks' clothes off and changing into my clothes, but the fear of someone recognizing me as a woman made me keep the clothes on. I couldn't help feeling uneasy. So I changed into a clean set of clothes I took from the sanctum.

Without turning on a lamp or a candle, I returned to my room and slept. For the first time in months, I didn't have a nightmare.

When I woke up the next day, I came out and began to search for familiar faces. Many people seemed to have left Zhenjiang already. I hoped that my family was one of those who successfully managed to escape, but I knew that had they gone anywhere near Nanjing, it would have been a certain death; if they had migrated, they'd have either died on the road from the cold and hunger, or be humiliated and persecuted by the Japanese soldiers... resulting in death.

I walked around for half the day. And then I found a familiar face far away, so I ran. It was Mrs. Han.

I soon caught up to her, and whispered, "Mrs. Han!" She looked at me for a moment before,

"Sel Lin? Are you Sel Lin?" recognizing me. I nodded and she immediately hugged me.

"Sel Lin... oh, Sel Lin... you poor thing... where in the world were you?" As she continued, my unease only multiplied.

"I... I was hiding in Nanjing..." and she replied, "You miraculously survived! That's so wonderful, ... so wonderful indeed...!" and began to tear up. I asked her,

"Do you happen to know about my family?"

"Your father passed away last winter. There was a small funeral in December. The Japanese military passed by this place. They kidnapped all of the girls! As for my daughter and Yul Lin...Ha Lin... well... I don't really know," and then Mrs. Han invited me to her house where she prepared as much as she could prepare to feed me.

Mrs. Han was living in the den of the store. Within it were piles of silk and clothes she used to sell. It seemed that the Japanese soldiers were unable to discover the place, which had led to it being preserved. She led me in, and gave me something to try on. As she gave me a sky blue qipao with pretty peonies sewed on it, and told me that she hoped for a day when I could wear this dress and roam the streets freely. She also prepared much food, and told me to take it home to eat there.

They were all delicious, yet I felt guilty enjoying them. My father after all, had passed away. The Japanese military had taken my sister, Yul Lin away, and there was no way of knowing what had happened to Ha Lin or Qu Lin. As the older sister, and the younger sibling, and the daughter who couldn't save any of them, I couldn't help but cry at my utter helplessness and incompetence. Although not the same as before, I wanted to live with my family again. But it was impossible. Just as the man in the cave had lost everything but his child, I had lost everything but my life.

I lived alone at my home for a while. I couldn't leave behind the house that was filled with items of my family. I managed to salvage some money while cleaning the house, and I used that money to survive alone. But I couldn't live like this forever. When the money ran out, I had to figure something out. Because of the war, many people living in Zhenjiang were homeless. After much thought, I decided to organize the house and put up some of the rooms for rent to the refugees. Because our house had many rooms that had been used by grandmother and grandfather as well as the rest of the family, I was able to not only manage, but even save some money.

I kept hoping that Yul Lin and my brothers would return home someday if I kept the house warm for them. But no matter how long I waited, they never came. More alarmingly, I'd been seeing more and more Japanese soldiers moving about my hometown. Whether my ability to sense had heightened since being in Nanjing or whether my belief in the Japanese soldiers being capable of inhumanely behavior had strengthened, all I knew was that I needed to avoid them. There was no way I could ever forget Nanjing.

A few months afterwards, the people that had been living at home left, and I cleaned the rooms out. Someone called for me from the outside. It was a man's voice.

"Hello? Someone here?"

As my heartbeat quickened, I quietly and carefully walked toward the main door. Since Nanjing, a man's voice would bring me fear, and made my hands perspire from nervousness. I quietly looked outside. There was a man wearing a priest clothing. I answered without opening the door,

"Who is it?"

He answered, "I am a priest passing by, and would like to find a place to spend the night."

I slowly opened the door. He had blond hair and blue eyes, and wore a black priest suit with white collar attached. He smiled kindly and said,

"Thank you for opening the door," and gave me a light bow. I also reciprocated and led him to his room. It was my brother, Ha Lin's room. He thanked me and entered the room. I told him, "Dinner is at seven."

"Is it? Thank you for telling me." He replied.

"Then have a good rest," and I closed the door for him.

That evening, I prepared dinner for the foreign priest who spoke excellent Chinese. He prayed and began to eat, while saying,

"This is amazingly delicious! It's been so long since I've had such good Chinese food!" and gulped the food down.

Soon after dinner, we began to talk. He said he had received assignment to work in Nanjing, and that although he'd normally travelled in China through rail, it was still a bit dangerous to do so.

"Of course, when there are so many refugees as it does now, it's very dangerous included train and anything else. Of course, I do look quite different from your average refugee," and laughed out loud.

As I looked at his innocent and bright smile, I found myself being caught completely unaware. These days, no one smiled like that. It had been so long. I then remembered the faces of all those who had lived here before the war; they had smiles like him. Although they'd worries about where their next meal would come from, they never stopped smiling. I remembered the pleasant hellos and even a bit of joshing about that my neighbors engaged in; I also remembered the times when especially, my father would smile brightly, as he exclaimed,

"A lot of customers came by today, so I've bought my little girls ribbons!" Walking in with little trinkets and gifts. Now, those neighbors were gone, and so was my father. The war turned our lives upside down, and the only thing left were empty ruined homes, open with their mouths wide open. Much like the corpses on the Yangtze...

The priest who quietly studied my face said nothing as he handed me a handkerchief. I looked at his hands, and he said,

"Dear sister, the people of this country has suffered much in the past and even now. But it will rise again. As long as one person believes there is hope, then the land as a whole has hope. I believe there are many people here in China who have hope, including you. Isn't that true? There is hope? Yes?"

As I heard sniffles, I realized I'd been crying. And I wiped my eyes with the handkerchief he offered when I'd realized.

"I don't know what exactly happened to you. But God loves you. He cares for you and wants you to be happy," said the priest. I could say nothing. I couldn't really believe his words. I lost everything. I saw what the Japanese had done, and their actions caused me a life of pain. How would his god bring me back my happiness!?

"What does your god know, that you can make such hasty comments?" I yelled, angrily. He hadn't done anything wrong, yet the way he talked, the way he looked; as if he knew brought out all of the repressed anger I'd buried deep inside.

He never got angry though. He continued without faltering.

"I don't know all of your pain. I don't know what kind of pain you endured. But God knows, and he will treat all of your pain. Of course, you'll have to open your heart to him."

Would I ever get my happiness and peace back? Could I feel happiness when at this moment in time, I knew nothing about the state of the rest of my family? Was it right for me to feel such things?

The priest spent a few more days at my house. He told me that he wasn't under duty to hurry to Nanjing. He told me that he'd like to learn a little more about Zhenjiang, and went outside early in the morning to walk around. I didn't know what he did when he went out. One day, he asked me how to get to the Yangtze River. I told him the directions, but he returned at night and told me that he'd gotten lost, and was unable to get to the River. Eventually, I promised to help him find the way the next day.

We woke up early next morning and walked the roads of Zhenjiang. I would warily glance at the Japanese soldiers walking with their guns. Whenever I passed by them, I hid behind the priest and walked a little closer to him, trying to hide myself from their view. Although he knew what I was doing, he said nothing.

When I arrived by the riverside, I couldn't believe my eyes. The small fish markets hugging the river no longer were there. The area was filled with homeless people, who all were begging. The priest walked over to them and handed them something. When I looked, it was a bit of food. He held their hands and listened to their stories, perhaps lessening the burdens in their hearts. It tugged at my heart strings.

That night, as we returned home, I asked the priest,

"I worry for their well-being; they can't find food, and could get murdered by the Japanese soldiers if they walk around wounded like that."

He answered,

"Man doesn't live on bread alone, does he, whether it's for his mind or body. China has a lot of natural resources. Everyone really wants this land. The land is big, and there are so many people here as well. If someone doesn't help their hearts heal, China will never be able to grow. Previous missionaries only wanted to enforce western ideas and refused to accept or understand China's way of life, but I believe that China must be respected in our efforts to enlighten them. So I volunteered to come here."

"How are you so good at speaking our language?"

"When I was young, I lived here with my father for a brief time."

We eventually walked back home.

In the alleyway, we met two Japanese soldiers who held rifles on their shoulders. They looked me up and down and gave a creepy grin. I unknowingly grabbed onto the arms of the priest, the hair on my back standing up in fear.

The priest did not look at me; he never took his eyes off of the soldiers.

One of the soldiers opened his mouth.

"Ah~ you must have had a nice night out~!" The soldier next to him gave a whistle and cackled.

"Our sister here and I were returning back after doing the Lord's work. The night out was with our God, ha ha ha."

"Sister? So you're a priest?"

He nodded and said that he was.

"Don't nuns usually have a special getup?" The man asked,

"Her clothes got dirty when we were working out by the river, so she had to change into this," replied the priest.

"Che~" Yet, because they didn't want to let us go, so we spent at least an hour at the alleyway trying to convince them of my "position." Priest Matthew finally managed to persuade them I was to be sent to England, and we returned home. As soon as we returned, he bowed down to me.

"I apologize for lying about you being a sister, but I wanted to help you."

I shook my head and lowered my head in response,

"Thank you for helping me."

He stopped himself several times, wanting to say something, before he finally let it out and said,

"I hope you'll listen to what I am saying carefully from now on. Please know that I don't say this easily."

I nodded.

"Won't you accompany me to Nanjing?"

"What…?"

The idea of returning to that hellish place made me hesitate. My head suddenly felt light, and I couldn't help but feel dizzy.

"I understand this could be a difficult request. But I saw you at the river today, as you were helping those people out. You looked so bright and alive. I'd been thinking about why I'd stayed here longer than I'd planned here at your house. I think the Lord has given me the answer. Perhaps the request to have you leave your home in Zhenjiang may be a shock for you, but I can't help but think that Nanjing needs you more."

I could say nothing. His sudden proposal made me speechless. He continued on.

"I can no longer stay in Zhenjiang. It is time for me to go to Nanjing, and I plan to do so on a horse cab. Next morning, if you prepare to leave with me, we shall go together, and if not, I shall leave on my own."

After he finished his proposition, he bid me good night and went into his room.

I found myself completely dumbfounded, and as I stared at the door he closed behind him, realized I would get no sleep that night.

Sixteen

Riverside Community, November, 2014

Hannah blinked several times. The eyes still burned, so she rubbed at them a few times. The papers Summer had left her were not in good condition. Some of the ink had run on the page; they were in Japanese, Chinese, and even English, which made translation utterly painful. Some of the pages were ripped, and she couldn't even bear to touch them before taping them up. Sel Lin's effort of writing throughout the most difficult part of the war astonished Hannah. How could have Sel Lin written all this during the turmoil?

Soon, Hannah's room became cluttered with pages of Sel Lin Chao's diary. As she had carefully laid each page out on the room, it was impossible to keep the window and the door open, which turned the room into a closed off space in no time.

Hannah couldn't take her eyes off of Sel Lin's writing. For someone like Hannah, who'd never been really interested in war, the inhumane behaviors of the Japanese soldiers made her gag for a while, and made her have nightmares about the terrors of war.

For the past month or so, Hannah almost never left the house. She felt compelled to read everything written on those tattered pages; she felt that she didn't have a lot of time.

Clint couldn't help but worry over Hannah's sudden obsessive and strange behavior, which was very different from her usual self. She didn't eat as regularly nor sleep as regularly; as her life turned less regular all around, he worried her health could decline. But there was nothing he could really do for her, and that made him even more uncomfortable.

Seventeen

Zhenjiang, June, 1938

The next morning, I left my home with the priest. We took a horse carriage to Nanjing, which only took a few hours. That long trip I had taken was of an unbelievably short distance.

We entered Nanjing. The city was still in utter ruin. It was worse than December. Corpses were everywhere, and only a handful amount of people walking around. Maybe it was because it was early summer, but the stink was utterly unbearable. I blocked my nose with the shirt sleeve.

There were crying children, beggars, and limbless people moving around while relying on wooden sticks. After what felt like forever, we finally managed to arrive at the convent. He got off and handed money to the carriage driver. He then knocked on the front door. After a moment, a voice replied,

"Who is it?"

"It is Matthew."

With the answer, the door opened and revealed a nun in her middle age.

"Ah, father Matthew, we waited a long time! Please do come in!" She invited us in.

Soon, she took us to the main office of the head nun. At the office of the head nun, Helen, the priest gave a simple explanation. Helen was a Dutch woman in her 40's and accepted me after hearing the priest's explanation. She said it was the toughest during Nanjing last winter. She then said it got much better in China since then, yet told me to be wary as Chinese people were not safe to move about. After telling me that it would take a few months before I could become a nun, she asked me why I wanted to be a nun.

I replied,

"I'm not entirely sure. These days, I don't know what my meaning in life is, nor what that means. But father here said I could do something here in Nanjing, and I followed him here."

She didn't say anything, but nodded, and led me to the dorm. I followed her steps up the stairs. Upon arrival, I found a few nuns working on clothes. The ladies there explained that they were making clothes for the orphans, who had surged in numbers recently. As it was difficult to obtain certain goods due to the war, they were cutting up old clothes of adults and curtains to make clothes for the children. And from that day on, I began to sew clothes for orphans and helped take care of the children at the convent. Most of the child care facilities were filled with war orphans, and some of them were with injuries, having been abandoned on the road. I began to smile more as I took care of the children. I also began to hope that the children would find their smiles once more as well.

Among my colleagues was a nun named Connie. She and I were of the same age. A 16-year-old girl, Connie was always incredibly quiet, so much so that most people wouldn't even remember her name. She helped out with all of the menial work at the convent, without a single complaint. After working with her for a few months, we went to our bedroom to turn in for the night. That night, I abruptly woke from sleep, hearing Yul Lin calling me, which made me fall nearly out of bed.

"ARGH!" My scream must have been so loud, as Connie woke up, surprised.

"What?! What is it?! Is it the Japanese?!"

"Yul… Yul Lin!" I gasped several times.

Connie held my hands tightly, as I began to sob out,

"I saw… my sister Yul Lin in my dream… she ran toward me… but… but…" I couldn't hold the sobs anymore. Connie then took me into her arms and hugged me tightly, while rubbing my back, quietly whispering,

"It's going to be okay, Sister Sel Lin. It's clearly the Lord's will that you will see your sister soon, don't you think? You must have been very surprised, right? It'll be all right, Sister Sel Lin…" and spent the rest of the night calming me down.

After that, Connie and I became very close, and we began to open up to each other. One random afternoon, while we took a break, Connie told me her story. She was going to attend Jinling University in the upcoming semester, and was living happily with her family, who was pretty well off at the time. Her father was a math professor at the university, and the house they lived in was passed down to them from her ancestor, where she'd lived with her family, including her grandmother and grandfather. On December 27th of last year, however, the Japanese soldiers arrived, committing rape and murder of everyone else in the family; she managed to survive by hiding in the small attic of their house. She told me I was the first one she'd told. I also told her of my story, of everything that had happened to me from December to March. She said that me being alive was such a relief, that it was all thanks to God; she said this as she tightly held onto my hands. We lived like so, relying on each other for support.

As the number of orphans grew exponentially, headmistress Helen gave out some of the nuns' bedrooms to other children. No one questioned her decision, but the tiny room the two of us had shared welcomed in two more sisters, and I couldn't help but feel a bit apologetic about sister Connie and my close relationship with her possibly causing discomfort to the other sisters. No one opposed headmistress Helen's decisions, however. Connie and I began to share our room with Deborah and Naomi. Deborah and Naomi were foreigners who worked with administrative work, and knew each other very well; of course, Connie and I who took care of the children also knew them. At first, our language barrier made it awkward for us at first, but we eventually warmed up to each other as we spent time together.

The time spent accepting the force called "God" was a more painful and confusing process. Evil things happen because of the devil. Yet the devil was someone God had treasured at one point. I couldn't understand it. Also, if God loved man so much, why did he allow such things to happen to Nanjing?

But there weren't a lot of time to truly ponder about these things. Twenty-four hours weren't enough to make the clothes, tend to the vegetable garden, and taking care of children. Perhaps my body was too tired; I didn't have too many nightmares, but when I did, I'd inevitably wake up everyone else in the room, and worry them with a fever. Thankfully though, they would nurse me back to health that I could move normally by morning.

Connie excelled at gardening. I usually took care of the new orphans, and watched over children aged five to thirteen with sister Maria, who was older than me. I taught the little ones how to read, while teaching the older ones the teachings of Confucius. Maria often said it was enough to teach them of the Bible alone, but I argued that if they didn't understand the culture and history of China properly, such horrible things would happen to China again. Sister Maria squealed on me to head mistress Helen, but father Matthew always defended me, stating,

"If we are to teach them the ways to salvation, we must do so in a manner that they can accept. We cannot go forth like we'd done in the past."

Maria scrunched up her face severely, but said nothing else to the matter.

After that, we taught both the Bible and Confucius, and did our best to explain the meaning of Catholic way of life as well as the spirit of China.

Early summer had passed by quickly, and it had already become late summer. Children came into the convent every day. Infants, injured children, children who looked smaller due to development issues, and children who seemed to be about seven years old or so. Some parents would abandon or leave their children with the convent orphanage, unable to feed and support them. They stood in line in front of me, wrote an application, and left their own child, or the child they found on the way by chance, or even their grandchild. That day was no different; I was busily registering children when I felt glances from a man. I looked up to meet his eyes and found I recognized his face.

"So you were a nun. It's great to see you. I was very curious," As I heard him, I lowered my head. It was the man who'd saved my life.

"Thank you so much for that time, sir. It is because of you that I'm here, working," I replied.

He smiled, slightly bitter, and wrote down Chung LeeQin on the application. He wrote Chung ShenLong for the name of the child. ShenLong was just a two-year old child. LeeQin explained that after Shanghai, he was unable to find any work, or a person who could look after the child, which prevented him from searching for any jobs. After spending the few months after his mother's death in the cave, he had a weak immune system; LeeQin said it broke his heart to see ShenLong be so weak. Since he wasn't in the situation to buy even the simplest medicine, he decided for the sake of the child, to leave the cave and ended up here, at the convent.

Connie took the ailing ShenLong from LeeQin, and took him to the hospital wing. LeeQin's eyes followed him until he and Connie disappeared from view. I asked what he planned to do, and he replied,

"I cannot give up on my child. Whether close or far, I will find work, earn money, and return to find ShenLong." He then bowed and turned away. I grabbed his sleeve quickly.

"If there is anything, I'd like to contact you and let you know. How long do you plan to stay in Nanjing?"

"I don't really have a place to go, but since a lot of empty houses are nearby,… I will try to visit everyday as soon as I find the time, also to see the baby. Please tell me then."

I bid him goodbye. Just as he had saved my life, I wanted to do something in return. That evening, Connie saw my uneaten food on the plate, and asked,

"Do you not have appetite?"

"How can I help Mr. Chung LeeQin?"

"Oh, the gentleman who came by this morning?"

"Mm-hmm…"

"Why are you so concerned?" Her face reflected her curiosity.

"He saved my life. He said he didn't want to give up on ShenLong. He said he was going to earn the money and come back for him. When you took him in earlier, his eyes never left him."

"But… a lot of people said the same thing before," replied Connie.

"True… but to him, there is only ShenLong. He lost everything in Shanghai, yet managed to hide away from the Japanese soldiers the past few months, raising ShenLong by himself while in hiding. I really think… if LeeQin earns the money… he'd figure out a way to raise ShenLong and come back for him."

Connie seemed to contemplate something as she leaned on chin on her palm. A moment later, she slapped her knee, as she shouted,

"I've got a great idea!" I carefully looked at her face.

"Sister Naomi told me that headmaster Helen had been making her do a lot of manual labor due to shortage of hands around the convent... but it's not like you can just bring any man inside, you know? To be honest, Father Matthew was never really a handyman. Since ShenLong is here as well, why don't we try recommending his father, LeeQin as a handyman to Sister Helen?"

Amazing! He was skilled enough to survive in a cave, and had even done work for the government in Shanghai at one point. As he was a farmer before all this began, he probably would have the skills to handle the work needed at the convent and the orphanage.

We talked to Naomi and Deborah about our plans, and they promised to ask Sister Helen, excited about the notions of no longer having to lift heavy things.

The evening after next day, Sister Helen called me. She asked me about Chung LeeQin.

"How did you meet him?"

"He saved my life," I answered truthfully.

"Saved you?"

"Yes. I tried to escape Nanjing earlier in the year, but slipped and was severely injured. If he hadn't saved me then, I wouldn't be here," I explained.

"I see..." she replied, "Right now, we're in need for someone who can take care of the convent and fix up the area. Compared to how much needs to be done, we lack helping hands, as well as money. Do you know where Mr. Chung is?" asked sister Helen.

I answered, "He said he's looking for a job, and would come see his son every day. He's probably out looking for a job right now. He'll come tomorrow."

Next day, Chung LeeQin came to inquire about his son's health as he'd promised. Sister Helen asked Connie and me to bring him to her. She asked him if he would be willing and able to carry on such rough work, to which he answered,

"Dear Sister, I've worked for the government in Shanghai, and while working as a farmer, had to leave everything and escape to Nanjing with my son. While the Japanese soldiers attacked and destroyed this city, I lived in a cave with my son. I only have ShenLong. I will do anything if that will guarantee a life for him. Give me a chance!" He yelled, while bowed low.

"We don't have a lot of money," Sister Helen replied,

" Is that going to be okay with you?"

"A place to live for my son and me is all I desire. I want nothing else," as he answered, I saw light and hope shining from his eyes, different from before.

Sister Helen gave him a storage space within the orphanage to live in. All he brought with him were mostly ShenLong's items and a few rabbit hides. He handed the rabbit hide to Connie and me, stating,

"I will get more later on, and let's have the children spend a warm winter!" He answered with a bright smile. And he began tirelessly to fix the side of the building that had fallen from the Japanese attack, gathering products, redrawing building plans, and getting ready to fix the building.

A few days later, ShenLong's fever went down, and LeeQin began his work. Connie became even better at farming thanks to LeeQin's tips, and by using compost, the vegetables began to grow even bigger.

When he had time, he never neglected to come see his son. I took care of ShenLong most of the time, and when I lifted him, his bright smile took away any darkness I felt within myself, and as if I were his parent, he followed me closely. Eventually, sister Helen gave me the name Marta, and at the entrance ceremony, I decided to give my life and heart to God. From then on, I was allowed to wear what other nuns wore. I was now Marta Chao, yet the memories as Sel Lin Chao remained. It was still painful and in disarray. Even if Christ the Lord washed away all my sins, he hadn't washed away my memories. I still knew nothing about Ha Lin, Qu Lin, nor Yul Lin's state; the nostalgia for the past never left, and I couldn't rip those feelings away. Whenever that happened, I'd hug the children tight, and when their tiny arms wrapped around me, I could feel a certain comfort.

Sister Helen called me one day. She told me that many people at the convent in Chongqing needed help, and that a few nuns including me would be sent over there. I returned to my room and began packing. The convent in Nanjing had opened its doors to many young women and those who were hurt and tired. Just like me, the women were given a way to survive and live with a purpose, as they became nuns and helped other sick and hurt people. Due to the high influx of nuns at our convent, we were able to divided our many tasks and handle them. Chongqing's inability to do so might have had to do with Sister Helen's understanding attitude. I had to leave here to go to a new place, not knowing when I'd return. Of course, the thought of leaving the children here did not comfort me at all. As I thought these things, I looked outside. LeeQin was fixing the window pane of an opposite building. I decided to say goodbye to at least him, and left my bags to go downstairs.

"Hello, LeeQin. I see you're very busy today as well," I said.

"Hello, sister Marta! Please wait a moment! I'll be right down!" He then came down to meet with me, leaving his work up top.

"Well, sister, I am here. Is there anything you wanted to say?"

"Yes. I will be going to Chongqing soon. I don't know how long I'll be staying there. I think I'll miss ShenLong the most, but Chongqing really needs help. So I'll be going tomorrow. I hope you'll be healthy," He didn't seem to be able to register the sudden goodbye, looking incredibly sad.

"Sister Marta, I will pray for your safe return every day. Don't worry about ShenLong or me, and be safe and healthy as well. I will continue to assist the head sister and other sisters as we protect this place," he replied.

I felt as if I could read his contemplative heart through his eyes.

As soon as I got up early that morning, I went to pray in the main sanctuary. I prayed for the many who would stay here. And most of all, I prayed for the safety of my two brothers and Yul Lin.

Then I took the train with sisters Connie, Katrina, and Julina. We sat facing each other, and quietly stared into each other's eyes as we began the long travel.

The train soon left Nanjing and continued west. During this time, Japanese soldiers would come in and thoroughly looked inside the cars, being careful and deliberate.

Once, they opened up the cornet and harassed us. Sister Julina, who was the oldest among us, warned them in Japanese,

"Please stop. We are on our way to take care of injured soldiers," and at this, the man who seemed to be of the highest rank, perhaps a lieutenant, stopped touching Connie's cornet, and gave a grin, looking at us. I was sitting on the inside, safe from their hands. But my legs were shaking inside the gown.

I don't know how many stations we passed. Some areas seemed completely uninhabited by people, and the Japanese soldiers looked out of their watchtowers with gun on their soldiers, standing by with solemn attitudes. The location wasn't too far from the railroad; the place where if I stretched out my hand, I could almost touch it; the place had smoke coming out of its chimney. The place was filled with the smell of burning hair. The sky over there was filled with smoke, reflecting a world of darkness. Sister Julina wordlessly closed the window and crossed her heart. I looked at her quietly.

As the evening Sun fell down into the river, we arrived at Yulhuan train station. From there, we took a ferry to Chongqing. Suffering from sea sickness as we rode on a ship for the first time, we looked up at the Yangtze river, and the world surrounding it. For the first time, I could understand why the world wanted this place.

Connie said, "We're currently on the backs of the dragon!"

I replied, "Then we could ascend into the sky!" Upon hearing this, sister Julina, who was known to be a stern and serious woman, smiled, before she crossed her chest once more.

The evening after that, as the Sunlight warmed up the river and took its last breath, we saw sisters waiting by the Chongqing harbor.

Eighteen

Chongqing, Autumn, 1940

Chongqing seemed more than big enough to work as Nanjing's replacement as the capital. Many people lived with the river in the middle, and all of their stories silently flowed with the river. More importantly, due to the recent intensifying of conflict between the Kuo Min Tang and the Communists, the hospitals filled up quickly, which led to the convent taking care of some of the lesser injuries as a result.

Through the grapevine, I heard of the Koreans operating in China, conspiring with the Chinese forces to repel the Japanese, and also for their own freedom, raising a young leader. Connie and I usually looked over children like before. A small number of young girls hid at the convent, in their attempt to escape the Japanese soldiers. They never said anything. But when they saw men, they shook, and were busy hiding if they heard Japanese or heard any story of the soldiers. I didn't know exactly what happened to them, but I tried to protect them from Japanese soldier the best I could, and I prayed for them. That was all I could do.

War leaves darkness in everyone. That darkness could swallow them at any moment. Connie, the sisters of Chongqing, and I were all trying to fight against darkness…, perhaps. We had no answer for war. If someone asked why war happens, we say that it is because people are evil. But… the basic question cannot be solved. Why God, who loves people so much, would give such pain. Perhaps pain comes to people because it is a way to show them their place, and God gives it to them so that people would come to him. Especially considering the fact that I was now living as a nun despite not knowing the "Je" in Jesus all my life. Perhaps it was the small lamp of light on those unable to see what is in front of them, as they fell, got hurt, or starved in the darkness. It wasn't a satisfactory answer considering my experience or knowledge, but thinking this way was the only way I could reduce the confusion in my heart.

The hospital has been lacking helpers lately. The convent began to send those with experience treating the wounded to the hospital, where the nuns would take care of them. Since I had some experience attending to the wounded in Nanjing, I went to the hospital twice a week, where I helped take care of patients, and where I comforted the dying, and prayed in their last moments.

That day was no different; I was on my way to the hospital with Connie. The hospital was a block away from the convent. Due to heavy bombardment from the Japanese air force, Chongqing was also feeling the destruction. Many wounded people were carried into the hospital every day. When we'd arrived at the hospital that day, it was nearly impossible to walk through the amount of people crowding the hospital. The patient who had been shot in the stomach and was bleeding profusely, armless people, legless people, and people with gunshot wounds on his head…we hurried onto the office to get our daily assignments. As I walked looking at the injured individuals, I stopped dead in my tracks. He looked to be Ha Lin. He seemed so like Ha Lin. He was my brother, Ha Lin. He was wearing the Kuo Min Tang uniform, and was on a stretcher, with a wound over his stomach. I didn't realize it, but I'd walked toward him. As I looked at him, I couldn't say a single thing. His face, filled with pain, seemed to recognize a shadow come over him. His scrunched face opened up, and his eyes widened. He tried to grab my hand as he stretched out his arm, and as I froze surprised, I realized he was straining. I quickly reached my hands out to grab his hands. We then went into the operation room together, and as the doctor tried to release my hand, Ha Lin refused to let go.

I told him,

"I will wait for you outside! Your sister Sel Lin will be waiting for you, so please come back out alive and well," and released my hands. His eyes never left mine as I left the operation room.

Connie soon found me, as I'd suddenly disappeared. She found me staring blankly at the operation room, and grabbed at my wrist. I looked at her.

"Marta? What's wrong? Why did you just disappear like that?"

But my shaking body, and red eyes made her worriedly ask,

"Are you all right? What's wrong?"

"My brother… Ha Lin…"

"What? Ha Lin?"

"My brother Ha Lin… he's in the operation room right now…" I choked it out. My throat was so dry all of the sudden. Once she understood, Connie's eyes widened in surprise.

"No… no way! Really?!" Surprised, we then both began to stare blankly at the operation room. Sometimes, we'd hear his scream, and I would be startled, cringing in pain. Overtime I did so, Connie held my hand tightly. We didn't know how long we'd stood there; from behind us,

"What are you doing at this busy time, sisters!?" a voice from the hospital manager surprised us. Connie explained to her of the situation, and asked to let me wait here until his operation was complete. She finally relented.

Connie tapped me on the shoulders a few times before going to work, and I continued to stand there, waiting for my brother. A few hours later, unconscious Ha Lin left the operation room and into a patient room. His body was wrapped in gauze. I asked the doctor of his status. He said Ha Lin had bled extensively, and that the removal of the bullet was a success. He said that we should look over him for the next few hours to see if he would become stable. He said the next couple of hours would be the toughest, but he should be okay if he survives it. I thanked him and had to return to work. Ha Lin was still alive, and there were people dying right now. As I worked the next couple of hours, I made sure to visit Ha Lin to check up on him. Sometimes, he'd groan and move about, rocking the bed. Whenever I saw it, I would change the towel on his forehead and held his hands tight. After awhile, he'd calm down, and breathe out, and I would quietly sing him the lullaby our mother used to sing for us when we were very young.

Because I was worried about my brother, I'd go visit his room whenever I had the time. I couldn't work like I normally did. When the evening came, Connie told me that she'd ask the manager about me staying the night with my brother, and I thanked her, promptly returning to his room.

I don't know how many days passed by since then. I was berated several times for not being able to carry on my duties as I usually did. That day was the same; I started my day near my brother's bed. When I looked up at the sound of the bedsheets moving, I saw my brother looking back at me. When our eyes met, I realized tears began to flow, unlike the first time we'd met again. We could say nothing, merely holding tightly onto each other's hands. He opened his lips first. I couldn't hear him too well, with his voice barely audible.

"Sel Lin... you're alive..., how amazing... ugh..."

"Don't force yourself, Ha Lin. To think you're up like this... oh thank the Lord!"

Ha Lin's nurse appeared then. She saw my brother and smiled brightly.

"Ah, you're awake and alive, Mr. Chao. It was a miracle that you're alive; had the bullet been just one centimeter to the left, you wouldn't be here right now."

I felt a shiver go down my spine. Ha Lin thanked her in a quiet voice. With that, I got up. With my brother finally awake, I realized the place was still filled with people dying. I was no longer Sel Lin. I grabbed his hand tightly one more, before getting up. I had to help others.

As a happy day began, the hospital began another busy day.

My brother showed fast recovery, and the hospital and the nuns couldn't hold their surprise. Ha Lin could now pull himself out of bed and go to the restroom by himself. He said he needed to find Qu Lin. He also wanted to find Yul Lin and bring her home.

After coming to Chongqing, as I visited my brother in the hospital, I continued to search for any information regarding Qu Lin and Yul Lin's whereabouts. Unlike Nanjing, Chongqing was a city with the culture of the mainland hidden deep within the country, unlike Nanjing. Maybe that was the reason, we would hear news of anti-Japanese movements gathering in the area through the grapevine of those in the hospital. Who may be a spy, who betrayed who, or even news of the soldier who tried to save a woman but failed and was prosecuted under live experimentation by the Japanese military committing experiments on live people... All kinds of rumors floated around.

I also heard that there were several such places located throughout China and Manchuria. Some said that tens of thousands of people had already died. Hospital employees often told them to save their energy healing, but they couldn't stop people from talking.

I couldn't help but think the Japanese had chosen to no longer be humans. How could a human being do this to another human being? But then I remembered the corpses, some with open stomaches, rotting corpses of babies in Nanjing, crowded by crows and other birds. The smell of rotting flesh is something I'd never forget.

I had no doubt that the Japanese could do all of these things. Then why did Yoshihiro keep me alive? Why was he so kind? I couldn't help but wonder. He'd kill his own soldier, and tried to save me until the end. What did he want? I still had so many unanswered questions.

Among the patients were those both from the Kuo Min Tang and the Communist Party, but while they were patients, they were just Chinese. Although I saw them debate fiercely several times. There must have been more fighting on the side of the Kuo Min Tang, when one considered the approximately three million soldiers fighting under Chiang Kai Shek, as they shouted for Communists to leave, and used unrelenting attack against them, or even putting them into traps.

Ha Lin tried his best to recover, saving his strength for the past few months. As I helped him out, I had many talks with him. He was different from before, of course. He told me that more than before, it was important for everyone to cooperate, to become one. He was convinced that the weakness of the Chinese caused the fall of Shanghai and Nanjing, that no one could truly capture the hearts of the people, and that the minds of the Chinese had become tainted with the Communist ideals from Russia. He was sure that such would lead to the downfall of China. He wasn't happy with me being a nun, but said that I would be a little safer than the average Chinese. I merely nodded. Although the Japanese were still horrible, it was nothing compared with Nanjing.

It took approximately ten months before Ha Lin finally recuperated. As soon has he recovered, he prepared to return to the battlefield. I wanted him to stay with me. I thought that if he stayed. Someday, we'd all reunite. I also worried that he'd get hurt once more, even further away. We'd finally met as it was…

I tried to convince him. I asked him to look after the injured soldiers at the hospital, and to help the orphanage out. He shook his head. He said he would return to the battlefield. I couldn't stop him. He said he could find more out about Qu Lin and Yul Lin if he went out. Even in the past, his stubbornness was well known in our neighborhood. So I stood by, helpless, hoping that he'd return safe and sound, as he rode away to battle once more under the early sunlight.

The fact that Ha Lin was of Kuo Min Tang did weigh heavily against my heart. More than theory, Kuo Min Tang soldiers have been harassing the convent, taking grains for their own use. The fight between the Japanese Imperial military, Kuo Min Tang, and the Communist had created a shortage in food for the orphans, yet the Kuo Min Tang soldiers ransacked the place whenever they came over. Sometimes, they would threaten the head mistress, noting that they received intelligence of Communists being hidden. It wasn't as if I couldn't understand Ha Lin, but I hoped he'd see his way and come back.

That day, I was looking over the orphans. The child's parents were murdered in a particularly horrific way by the Japanese soldier, which had caused a trauma in him; he was unable to speak properly. I spent extra time with him in order to help him, and gave him special lessons.

"Here... Kyoo In, ... butterfly. This is a butterfly."

"Ooh... boo...!" I didn't know what kind of trauma he had suffered, but unlike other children, Kyoo In's inability to verbalize even a word made me worry significantly.

"Kyoo In, here... Bu, say buh-. buh."

"Boo. Boo... oh... ah!"

"Good! Let's try again. Buh-. then utter~ that's right, open your mouth like that! Who is this brilliant kid, Kyoo In? You're so great!" Could it be because I smiled brightly at him, he made a cute noise as he squealed and giggled.

On one hand, I worried for Kyoo In, who was so behind everyone else, yet if this wounded soul could feel happy for even a little moment, and if I could help him heal, I wanted to do what I could, so that he could get along with other children and grow up to be a healthy happy member of society.

As I concentrated on Kyoo In's pronunciation and word studying, I could see Connie rushing toward me.

"Sister Marta!" She gasped for air as soon as she arrived, and eventually leaned on her knees while she caught her breath. I waited until she caught her breath.

"We found her!" Connie grabbed my shoulders and said those words. I didn't know what she meant by it, so I looked at her. Kyoo In was quietly holding onto my skirt, and looked up at us.

Apparently, Ha Lin had shown one of the soldiers a photo of our family, and someone in the hospital recognized Yul Lin, saying he'd seen someone looking like her before. Ha Lin had a photo of my family when father was still alive with him, which he used to inquire about the family's whereabouts. He had taken the photo with him when he left to join the Kuo Min Tang once more. Connie and I left Kyoo In with sister Sarah, and hurried towards the hospital. When I arrived at the hospital, I could feel excitement build up in my heart as I looked for the patient.

"Mr. Yuian Yang?" Connie walked up to the patient. His left face and head was wrapped in gauze, and he smiled when he saw us.

"Ah! It does seem like the girl in the photo and you look alike. I saw you and felt that it was very familiar, but it was only yesterday that I was finally able to place the face," he said, looking at my face. My heart beat even faster.

"So what happened to her?" My voice was surprisingly shaky.

"I'm not too sure... at the time, she was found with two Korean women. One of the woman died from heavy bleeding while on the way to the hospital wing,... and... I can't be sure I know what happened to her. I was on a mission, so I couldn't keep up with them.

"Where... where is that place?" I hoped both that it would and would not be Yul Lin. To think that she was found with a woman who died from too much bleeding...? What had happened to her?!

"It was near Nanjing... but I'm not sure she'll still be there. As you know, Nanjing is still unsafe, yes? It's not the most comfortable place for vulnerable women... wouldn't they have moved onto a safer location?

"Is... isn't there... a way to know... where that person may have gone to...?" as I asked, I could feel heat coming up my eyes.

Yuian seemed to be lost in thought before he gave a light thump with his fist on his palm.

"Isn't there a Kuo Min Tang headquarters in Chongqing? Wouldn't they have some sort of a record there?"

Connie and my eyes widened in surprise. Without intending to do so, in a loud voice, I yelled,

"You're right! There was such a method!" and thanked him, bowing several times. He said that it was okay, and told me to hurry on ahead. That night, Connie and I stepped by the head mistress' office to explain my situation. At first, head mistress was hesitant, as she said,

"You've already promised your life to the Lord. Yet you're saying that you will leave this place for the night, just to check up on your old family?"

I explained,

"I just wanted to verify that my sister Yul Lin is still alive. That's all I wanted to check. Once I figure out her status, I think I could devote my life to God even more," and begged her.

Connie also begged, "Sister, please help sister Marta serve the lord better!" and she begged, as if she were begging to find out about her own family.

Finally, she relented. That night, Connie and I went to the bus station by the Yangtze River, where a bus carried people across the river to the other side. To think Zhen Jiang nor Nanjing had such a system made me realize why Chongqing made sense as a new capital, and why people gathered here. Chongqing had media outlets for both the Kuo Min Tang and the Communists, and was home to at least fifty embassies. It was also a city filled with Koreans engaging in anti-Japanese movement. As many cultures mixed and clashed, we were able to see all of the conflict play out in the media. Even if most of the city was in ruins due to the Japanese bombardment, and the roads were filled with the corpses and wounded bodies of people from last night's bombing.

We took the bus into the city and arrived at the Kuo Min Tang's personnel office. On the red bricked building held the flag of the Kuo Min Tang, waving in the air.

Beyond the desk was a man in a uniform, but it was as if the clothing could not cover him completely; this was visible through his rather thin hands. He wore the name tag Hai Yun Tsen.

He looked at our clothes briefly before asking, face filled with curiosity, "What brings you here?"

I cleared my throat and replied, "I would like to know about my sister's whereabouts. Her name is Yul Lin Chao, and I was told that she was found in Nanjing a few months back. I would like to know where she is now," and upon hearing it, he told me to wait a while, and went over to the man sitting at the largest desk in the deepest corner of the office, where they had some sort of a conversation. Then he lifted his phone. A few moment later, he came over to me, and told me to sit and wait.

A few moments later, a woman walked toward us. She wasn't Yul Lin; I'd never seen her before.

"Hello, my name is Sun-Soon Kim; I am from Chosun. I hear you're here to find Yul Lin Chao?"

I nodded, fear beginning to creep back up and preventing me from talking.

She gave a deep sigh before turning over to Hai Yun Tsen, and saying, "I will be out for a moment, so if anyone looks for me, let them know as such," then turned around to direct us to the door, where she said, "There is a tea house nearby. Would you like to go with me?"

My chest felt as if someone had placed a large boulder on it. Why did someone else come out when the person I'm looking for was Yul Lin? So Connie, Sun-Soon, and I visited the nearby tea house. She ordered wu long tea and said,

"I have something to tell you about Yul Lin Chao."

I sat across from her. Connie quietly sat next to me. We exchanged pleasantries briefly, and then Sun-Soon sat wordlessly until the tea came out. I quietly watched her fingers as they moved on the table.

Soon, the tea came out, and Sun-Soon finally opened her lips after taking a sip.

"Could I ask you how you met Yul Lin? I'm her sister, as you may have heard from Mr. Tsen."

"I wouldn't say how we met is nearly as important as how we separated. You're her sister, ah, I see." Sun-Soon's face darkened.

Sun-Soon's divisive manners annoyed me, as she kept circling around the important issue. I finally came forth as I demanded the truth.

"I came here to learn about the whereabouts of Yul Lin. Why did you come out?"

Her shoulders shuddered before she finally confessed,

"Yul Lin... Yul Lin… passed away a month ago," The tea cup fell from my hand, and hit the table, spilling the slightly cooling tea on the wooden surface. Connie quickly set the cup straight, and wiped it down with a towel nearby.

The hopeful maybe completely disappeared, leaving me in ever deepening abyss of despair. I couldn't even cry, so completely in shock.

She passed away, not having lived a life at all.

"How... how could this happen...?" Connie asked Sun-Soon. Sun-Soon spoke, shaking her head.

"The Japanese soldiers held us captive near Nanjing. We did everything we were told and lived in constant fear of death for several years," she took another gulp of wu long tea.

"Then we heard about the Japanese soldiers mention the Kuo Min Tang organizing to retake Nanjing. So… five of us, including Yul Lin and I, decided to escape that place, planned our escape, and acted on it."

"But the Kuo Min Tang only found three…" at Connie's inquiry, Sun-Soon shook her head.

"Two were probably killed by the Japanese before we got away… I still remember the sound of gunshots behind me."

For the first time, I took a good look at Sun-Soon. Her voice was strong. But when she talked of the two women who'd probably been killed, her voice began to shake slightly.

Her eyes met mine, and she dropped her eyes, unable to look at either Connie or me; and she continued.

"To be honest, Yul Lin and Gyoung-Ja weren't healthy. Gyoung-Ja told us to leave her at one point. Thankfully, Kuo Min Tang soldiers found us… but… by then… it was already too late for Gyoung-Ja." Sun-Soon quickly rubbed her eyes. Then she rubbed her hand on her clothes. "Truthfully, I didn't even realize how bad Yul-Lin's state was. But as soon as we arrived at safety, she collapsed… and didn't wake up once."

She then carefully placed her empty tea cup on the table. I looked at her hands on the table, mindless. Surely, I was shaking in despair and sadness, my own body shaking from the shock of never seeing my sister Yul Lin… yet Sun-Soon had lost all of her friends. Being the sole survivor from a promise to escape must have been a giant burden on her, yet Yul Lin's death mattered more to me than her difficult situations.

I carefully bowed my head. Then I opened my mouth to say,

"I see that I was rude just now. It wasn't your fault, but I feel that I've pushed you onto an edge. I am sorry."

Sun-Soon smiled bitterly and shook her head. "No, sister. I don't know if you'd believe me, but I understand your sentiment. I lost not only my country, but all of my family," At her words, I realized the limits of my ability to understand the other's pain, and began to feel sorry.

"What do you…?"

"I don't have parents. I used to have an older brother… but the Japanese took him away and then took me away. I don't even know if my brother is alive or dead."

Unknowingly, I grabbed onto her hands, which were still wrapped around the empty cup. Surprised, she looked up at me. I couldn't say a word of condolence. But I looked into her eyes directly. She was an orphan, who'd lost all of her family, and lived an unknowingly difficult life, yet she was alive here. The three of us sat there, in the small corner store located behind bombarded crumbles of the street, wordlessly; in that teahouse in Chongqing, surrounded by people hurrying home.

Nineteen

Chongqing, August, 1943

It's been nearly a year since Ha Lin left for war. He hadn't sent me a single letter, and I worried about him. As I'd already lost a sibling, I hoped even more that Ha Lin and Qu Lin would be safe.

After meeting with Sun-Soon that evening, I returned to the office to ask Hai Yun Tsen to help me send a letter to Ha Lin Chao. He agreed to do so, and I wrote a simple letter.

Ha Lin,

I hope you're doing well.

Yul Lin is no longer in this world, but do not despair; please continue to search for Qu Lin. I shall do the same.

I await your response.

Marta

From then on, I met Sun-Soon more often. The woman who was with Yul Lin's last moment was an orphan. She was a determined woman, who'd survived and won over that darkness. But when we talked, I couldn't help but feel a certain wall. I knew she was hiding something, but I had no way of knowing what that was. But I also felt incredibly sorry for her; if it was something that she'd protected that much to hide, I didn't want to force it out of her. There seemed to be a fear that if I did open that wall, we'd end up completely lost in that darkness hiding beneath.

I also continued visiting the hospital everyday to see patients. There were still many soldiers suffering from injury, and after meeting with Sun-Soon briefly, I took the bus back to the convent. I couldn't help but feel someone following me. I stopped and looked back. No one was there. But my senses were telling me otherwise, and intuitively, I knew not to trust what I saw only. I quickened my pace. Once I arrived at the convent, I quickly opened the door and went in. It was only after I locked the door, did I breathe with ease.

These things happened more often, and I couldn't get rid of the fear that someone was following me. As a result, I met Sun-Soon a little less and spent more time at the convent. As for the hospital, I tried to arrive and leave the hospital early. I could then lessen such ominous feeling. Although it didn't last for too long.

One day, I returned extra early from the hospital, and was on my way back to the convent. As I walked, someone walking on the opposite side tapped my shoulders slightly with his, and as I couldn't erase that ominous feeling, I stopped and looked back. There were many people walking on the road. But then a familiar back caught my eyes. He was wearing civilian clothing. The style of walking or behavior didn't seem similar, … but his height or feeling seemed familiar. I stood there watching his back get smaller and smaller. He never turned around, continuing to walk away, and soon disappeared from my sight. But I knew. It was the lieutenant in the Japanese army, Yoshihiro Saito, the Korean man who saved my life.

After that incident, I no longer felt the constant feeling of being followed. Perhaps Yoshihiro meant to say hi. On one end, I felt a certain feeling of positive recognition at the man who saved my life, but the words that described the group he was associated with, the Japanese military, was now synonymous with cruelty, inhumanness, and its actions were deemed too horrid to be considered normal. I couldn't help but remember the events by the Yangtze River whenever I saw a Japanese soldier. I couldn't help but feel anger boil up when I thought of Yul Lin, who died at their hands, and of the soldiers who'd violated me, now bugs torturing me deep inside.

Around August, Sun-Soon came to see me at the convent.

"Sister Marta," the eyes of the woman who was the same age as me was shining brightly.

"Sun-Soon, what's going on... is today your off day?" I took her to the guest room.

"What tea would you like?" I asked Sun-Soon, and as I began to search, she said,

"I plan to leave Chongqing."

The thought of tea forgotten, I was caught completely by surprise.

"What are you talking about? Go where?" I sat myself down in front of her and looked at her; nearly drilling a hole in her face with my stare.

"China hasn't fallen to Japan yet," answered Sun-Soon. "But... my motherland... is Japan's. I must save my country from the hands of the Japanese. I don't want any more people to end up in my situation because of Japan," the glares from her eyes hid a strong determination.

I didn't make any effort to stop her. A country without strength will force a fate worse than hell for its people. Weren't Yul Lin, Sun-Soon, and I all an example of that? But as we'd relied on each other heavily, I couldn't let go of a certain feelings of regret. I said truthfully,

"I will miss you much, Sun-Soon. But I don't have any desire to stop you. I hope you succeed, and I hope to see you alive." She smiled brightly at me.

"Thanks, sister Marta."

We said our goodbyes like that. I hugged Sun-Soon tightly, and stood there until she disappeared from sight.

She would no longer be a Kuo Min Tang nurse, but a member of the Choson Militia member. All I could do was pray for her safety and survival in this crazy world.

Problems were continuing to exist with Kuo Min Tang. As they had many members, the members of the Kuo Min Tang wreaked havoc on the people of the neighborhood. It wasn't that we couldn't understand them. Kuo Min Tang apparently used a method of burning the land and houses when fighting the Japanese Imperial Military. As a result, food became scarce, and the inability to provide adequate food to the soldiers probably made it difficult to keep the soldiers from being comfortable. But the civilians also needed food to survive; thus it was also understandable that no one truly could welcome in the Kuo Min Tang, when they would threaten the civilians for food and money.

Like other days, the men who claimed to be Kuo Min Tang soldiers had wasted away our morning, wreaking havoc in the convent, and head mistress Esther had spent all her energy arguing with them.

Yet the energy on the streets of Chongqing was alive. There were news of Japanese defeat filling the streets, and the newspapers reported on the inevitable end of the war coming soon. I asked around, wondering about it. Mr. Wang, who ran a noodle shop near by convent said,

"England and America is helping China push back Japan! These days, Japanese Imperialists are running away, tails between their legs!" and continued, "Once this war is over, we'll never have to worry about bombs in Chongqing, and sleep without worry!" and laughed brightly. Connie and I also smiled back before making our way to the hospital.

It did seem as if the Japanese soldiers were pushing on their last hoorah. After Nanjing fell, the Japanese were heavily bombarding Chongqing continuously. Due to the Japanese air force's constant bombings, many of the important buildings in the city were crumbling. Hospital was always filled with patients: people injured from the bombings and the people from the battlefield. Compared to the amount of patients, those qualified to help were always shorthanded.

I had to go to a hospital located a bit further away. Last night, the hospital had requested help. Head mistress Esther asked Connie and me, and we accepted without a doubt. As we talked about this and that, we began our walk toward the hospital on the outskirts of the city.

The hospital was jam packed. No, it was beyond being jam packed; the hospital was overflowing with patients. Hospital manager Dao Qing ran toward us and thanked us many times. He immediately took us to the intensive care unit. The inside of the room was appalling. Some of the patients were from Burma. Eastern port cities were all under Japanese control, so most of military equipments and shipments came in through a supply line in Burma. Connie made an off-handed comment about there being a battle by Burma.

We moved the most severe cases to the surgery room and helped with surgery preparation, and helped the nurses dress those who were done with surgery. By the end of that night, we ended up sleeping in a small room at the hospital, due to working so late.

We returned the next evening, and the Japanese bombardments started that night. We heard a bomb crash nearby, and surprised, we ran out of our beds and began to run toward the underground shelters.

"Everyone! In three lines! Hold your hands!" head mistress yelled out loudly. As I walked out with the children, I realized Kyoo In was nowhere to be seen.

I yelled out for Kyoo In.

"Kyoo In! Kyoo In! Have you seen Kyoo In? Wait... Kyoo In! Kyoo In!" I tried to run back into the building, but Connie grabbed my arm and said,

"Let's hurry to the shelter! I'm sure Kyoo In is there!" and dragged me out.

As I was about to leave the building, I heard a familiar cry. It was Kyoo In. I pulled Connie's arm away and said,

"I'll bring Kyoo In. You go first. Wei seems to be having trouble walking, take him and wait for me there, okay!?"

Connie looked between Wei and me before running toward Wei. I ran back into the building. Searching every room, I ran down the hallway for Kyoo In, and heard another loud "boom!" nearby as a bomb dropped. I opened every door, and finally, in the third room from the back, I found Kyoo In crying near the window, who had been looking outside.

I ran in, "Kyoo In!" and Kyoo In turned around hearing my voice. He raised his arms at me, and I picked him up before running outside. As I neared the exit, a bomb fell right in front of me. From the impact, cracked sidewalk pieces flew at me, and as I tried to protect Kyoo In by turning away, I suddenly felt heat on my left cheek and arm, and fell to the ground. Kyoo In began to cry, surprised from the sudden impact.

When I got back up, I found my right leg refusing to move. I dragged one leg, and held Kyoo In on one arm, and began to crawl out of the exit. I passed by the exit, and managed out of the main exit beyond the back yard. I pushed the door, and saw a few neighbors who recognized me and helped me to the shelter. We went to the nearest underground bomb shelter and arrived. We all spent the night, our eyes wide open, as the bombs crashed all over our world. My legs were bleeding and cut. A piece of the rock must have had hit my leg; I would need help of others to function. A neighborhood lady who had helped me into the shelter ripped the ends of her skirt and tied it around my leg. Thankfully, the injury wasn't very deep, but it was important to stop the bleeding nevertheless. Most importantly, Kyoo In was safe. He was uninjured. It was a relief.

Next morning, everyone who had hid in the bomb shelter all came outside. I limped out, with the help of people. The convent that was fine until last night was burning. Connie ran over to me and hugged me tightly, and I reciprocated.

Connie then saw the dried blood on my cheek and arm, and the limping on my right leg, and with surprise, yelled out,

"Sister Marta! You're hurt!?"

I rubbed lightly at my cheek and winced at the pain. Connie looked me up and down carefully and said in a worried voice,

"What are we going to do… the injury is a lot deeper than it looks!"

"This much is doable." I replied, smiling back. When I smiled, the pain on my cheek worsened. Connie brought an emergency medical care box, sanitized my face, arm, and leg, and put on medicine before wrapping with gauze.

"But… I'm still alive, right?" I said. She nodded in response.

Covered in dust, she and I looked at the location where there used to be our convent. Next to me was Kyoo In, holding tightly onto my pajama pant, mumbling something. It seemed that I had severely sprained my ankle as well. It was then that I realized not only had I sprained my ankle, but where I had hurt my leg was more severe than I'd once thought.

The smoke filled the spring sky in Chongqing, and the groans heard here and there made it feel as if we were heading into a foggy maze.

Twenty

Riverside Community, December, 2014

These days, Hannah was unable to work or write poetry due to the heightened
level of stress. She had finished most of the organization on Sel Lin Chao's diary,
and translated the pages in Chinese and Japanese into English. She'd carefully
placed the diary pages into a clear file to prevent further decay or ruin and to
preserve them.

The wretchedness of war couldn't have been learned at school after all. Hannah
had never learned about the Sino-Japanese war in school. She only learned about
the Japanese invasion of Manchuria during World War II, and that the Japanese
had committed the Nanking Massacre. Of course, had she read Sel Lin Chao's
diary at that age, her friends and she would have been scarred for life at the images
and lives of those who'd become a sacrifice of Imperialism, the end of those
who'd turned traitor to survive, and of the hatred and shock about human beings.

Hannah pondered. Where would the line between learning and protection be?
History unlearned repeats. Would the children have to learn such horrific past,
bearing the danger of what it could do to their psyche? And the adults? How many
adults truly knew of the lives of such people? Was it okay to live inside one's own
little cocoon, not knowing of the pain of all those who suffer? Is there a Nanking

Massacre happening somewhere else on the planet? Don't we live in content ignorance, sure that we know from all we hear and see? To be honest, learning about the past was torturous, but through the process that was learning, shouldn't we prevent such thing from happening again?

Many thoughts tangled inside the head. Then she suddenly wondered. Did someone named Sel Lin Chao actually exist? There was no identification or birth certificate. Summer had left Hannah the diary, as if it were her last letter, or perhaps like Anne Frank's diary, a way to communicate her thought to the outside world.

Therefore, it was important to Hannah as well. Yet if it were a novel written by some Chinese person from the past?

Hannah would say that the story was a great fiction. With these papers alone, Hannah could not prove the true or fictional existence of Sel Lin Chao. Also, as Hannah still didn't understand the purpose behind Summer's intent in leaving this to her, Hannah couldn't help but wonder even further, as to exactly what Summer wanted from her.

Nevertheless, Hannah continued to translate and read. She believed that once she read through everything, she could find some answers. She couldn't sleep, and she had no appetite. All she wanted to do was continue to organize the papers.

Hannah soon lost all of her weekends. Day and Night no longer made much impact. If she were tired, she slept, and if she woke, she worked on the documents. The house began to collect dust in the corners, and without airing out the house, the curtains blocked sunlight from entering the house. Clint once complained of coming home to a dark and dusty house, angered at Hannah. But every time he did so, Hannah replied,

"It's to reduce the danger."

"What is so dangerous? If it's a thief issue, we've installed a home security system, and there's even the prevention system."

"No… we still must reduce the danger," said Hannah, stubbornly.

Clint worried for Hannah's state. As Hannah had never been so deeply involved with anything, Clint felt as if he'd met someone completely unfamiliar in his own home.

As Hannah lived in her study, Clint looked at her with worry and frustration. What kind of a person was Summer Wu, that she shook Hannah's life so? Since Clint still had to leave for work early, he tried to come in as early as possible.

Every time he came home, he was facing a sink full of dirty dishes, dusty living room and bedroom, and the thick dark curtain blocking out any light. Eventually, he snapped.

He stomped over to the study, expecting to see Hannah.

"Hannah! I'm home…!"

But Hannah wasn't inside. Clint felt his heart drop.

The light in the room was still on. Clint closed the door and looked around the house, but Hannah wasn't home. Worried, he called her cell phone, and found the phone ringing inside the house; she'd left her phone at home.

What had prompted her to leave the house without her phone, when she'd basically been a hibernating bear these days?!

Clint went back out and picked up his key outside. As he got in his car, he saw Hannah's car come in. With a sigh of relief came the uncontrollable anger. Once Hannah parked her car inside the driveway, his emotions exploded.

"Where the hell were you, leaving your phone at home!?" yelled Clint, enraged.

Hannah dropped the Chinese take out in her hands, startled.

"Di… dinner…" replied Hannah, still flustered.

Clint brushed at his hair, and gave another deep sigh. Then he walked over to Hannah and picked up the plastic bag with the food. She must have not purchased any stew, as the food did not leak out of the bag.

She was still frozen, and Clint brought Hannah in, holding her hand.

"I've been worried due to the change in your behavior. When I'd come home, I couldn't find you anywhere… you weren't in the study," as Hannah looked at Clint, she realized her mistake…a-cha! She should have at least taken her phone…

Apologetically, Clint took the food and placed it on the table. He then took the plates out of the kitchen cabinet and placed them on the table, before setting the spoons and forks as well. Hannah quietly thanked him, and took the food to her mouth, before looking at the table blankly.

Clint gulped down the food, unexpectedly hungry. Afterwards, Clint saw Hannah moving the romain on her plate around, her chin on her hand.

"Aren't you eating?" asked Clint,

and Hannah continued to stir her food around, as if she'd heard nothing.

"Hannah. Hannah?" Clint called her several times, and she blinked a couple of times before looking up at Clint.

"Ah... yes. Sorry."

"What's with you these days? Are you all right?"

Hannah hesitated for a while before finally opening her mouth.

"For a fiction to become real, what is necessary?

"About what..." Clint fell into thought, then said. "Is it related to Summer Wu?" At Hannah's silence,

"So it is,"

as Clint verified his own answer, his face filled with annoyance.

At this, Hannah couldn't help but feel angry.

"No, don't worry about it. I'm not hungry yet, so I'm just going in,"

Hannah got up and tried to go back to her study, but couldn't due to Clint's response.

"What did Summer Wu do for you? Why is the study cluttered with pieces of paper? I understand she mattered a lot to you. But you're being so weird. Are you even taking care of your health at all?"

Hannah turned around to look at Clint. His eyes were genuine, and reflected how much he'd worried about her. Hannah returned to the table, and held Clint's hands, which were sitting on the kitchen table.

"Thank you for worrying about me. You're the only one," said Hannah.

"I'm just worried about you. You've never been like this," replied Clint, lightly rubbing Hannah's hands.

"Being passionate is good... but shouldn't you also care about your health?"

Hannah stared at Clint for a moment before smiling and answering,

"Yes… I'm sorry. But… I have to finish this. I know you'll understand. Even I didn't realize how important Summer was in my life. Once I have all of the answers, I'll definitely tell you. Please trust me."

Clint nodded, clearly unsatisfied.

"Yes… I'll trust you."

That night, Hannah didn't go back into the study, but instead went to bed with Clint, where she got a deep night of sleep for once.

Twenty One

Chongqing, July, 1944

The burning sunlight of the summer, dust, and the news from the north was disastrous. Japan as on the attack again. Through Beijing. Of course, Chonqing was very far from Beijing, and Japan was still on the coastline, but they were fast. So I couldn't calm down.

Thankfully though, bombardment stopped, so the buildings in Chongqing were being rebuilt and the convent was nearly fixed. Collapsed convent building last year still brought painful memories.

After that event, my arm had a small burn mark, and on my leg was a deep gash which showed how serious the injury was. On my left cheek was also a deep cut. Thankfully, my ankle was fully healed, so I didn't have too much problem working or carrying on with my life.

These days, the word around the grapevine was that the Kuo Min Tang and the Communists were criticizing each other and trying to find loopholes in each other. Due to Ichigo Sakusen's success in China, the Communist soldiers and Kuo Min Tang soldiers were blaming each other, or so, said Mr. Wang, as he poured the noodle into the bowl. I couldn't help but worry; it would be difficult if they cooperated, yet they were fighting...

If I had to choose between the two though, I would choose the Communists though. Although there were less of them, they were ethical and never threatened civilians for food or items. Although it was relatively simple idea, I wasn't the only one thinking this way. One time, I met a Communist supporter. He had gone to USSR to study abroad, and returned when he found out about the state of China. He and his friend protected the civilians against Kuo Min Tang soldiers and criticized Kuo Min Tang's tendencies to enter homes and take whatever they wanted, as well as their tendency to commit all kinds of injustice and irrational behavior. From then on, those in the neighborhood and other civilians beginning to support Communism was an obvious result.

One day, I saw a familiar face outside of the convent. We hugged each other, excited to see each other. Her sharp eyes seemed to embody that of a soldiers, and I felt comforted by it.

She told me that she was now an official soldier of the liberation army.

"You wouldn't know," she said.

"Know what?" I asked her.

"The feeling of fighting for my country, I feel like I'm now truly a human being. Although the training makes me want to die sometimes... but if I can live as a citizen of Choson, I can do and give whatever I have!" Her confidence, to be honest, made her so cool.

"You've really become so cool," I said, and she blushed and gave me a bright smile, "Really? Hearing it does embarrass me a bit though," the replying face of Sun-Soon looked truly happy. I couldn't help but smile back, slightly aware of how I compared with this confident woman, who was the same age as me: twenty-two.

Sun-Soon couldn't stay long. She was here to work. She explained everything to me while we had a cup of tea. She found and went to the liberation army after saying goodbye to me. They took her to Beijing, and from there, she did everything from transferring money to working out by the enemy lines.

"One time, a grenade flew in front of me! I threw it back out totally on reflex! I don't even know where such a crazy behavior came from!"

I took another sip as I listened to her exciting story. She then looked and me and asked,

"That injury on your cheek... what happened?" I also explained to her what had happened to me that night at the convent. She said,

"Oh, that's so lucky that you're alive! Really, fortunate!" She said as she held my hands tightly.

After that, we went our separate ways, and I returned to my normal life. Strangely, after that incident, Kyoo In began to talk. When he saw me, he'd say, "Shi-stah~" and showed he recognized me, and even hung out with other children. At first, they made fun of him for the way he talked. However, his bright smile and tenacious nature eventually won the hearts of all of his friends.

After a while, Chung LeeQin family came to see me. Since I left Nanjing, LeeQin lived in the convent with his son ShenLong, and helped out with all of the outside work. As the convent hired more people, LeeQin was able to take breaks. LeeQin had sent me countless amount of letters. He told me of sister Helen's well being. He said that his health was failing, but he'd wanted to show Chongqing to his son, and to discuss something with me, and that he'd make effort to come see me.

To meet him, I made my way to the port. As I saw the ship come in, I realized I was excited to see them. As the father and son walked toward me, I recognized just how big ShenLong had gotten. ShenLong blinked his big eyes a couple of times before running toward me and running into me. His soft cheek met mine. I hugged him tightly. His long thin eyes and puffy cheeks made him look so innocent.

Chung LeeQin came over to me and said hello. I bowed to reciprocate. As we walked slowly, he told me,

"My health hasn't been very good, so the hospital recommended I find time for myself."

I could say nothing. LeeQin's face was rather dark. He winced every once in a while but did not show himself as being sick.

As soon as we arrived at the convent, we said hello to the head mistress, and sat down at the reception room with a cup of tea prepared by the head mistress.

"I hope you didn't have trouble coming all this way. Will you then be living in Chongqing from now on?"

He nodded,

"Sister Helen has already received permission from the head mistress here in Chongqing." He then said seriously, "Sister Marta, thank you so much for helping me all this time. I do apologize for having to ask you for yet another request."

"No, it's fine. Please go on."

"The doctor told me that I probably won't last more than a couple of months. He told me to wind down everything and take care of them."

I was caught completely unaware. LeeQin did look ill, but I didn't think it would be to this extent. He said,

"I wanted to do my best to support ShenLong until he became an adult, but my body doesn't seem to want to support it anymore. Since I can't ask anyone else, I sought to seek your help out. To be honest with you, that is why I am here. Will you help me?"

"I don't know whether I will be able to stay here or whether I will be assigned elsewhere. So I can't guarantee anything, but while I am here, I will do what I can. As I am a nun, I cannot simply look over ShenLong alone, so if you can understand that, I will look over him,"

He seemed satisfied with the answer, as he repeatedly thanked me.

That evening, I brought Mr. Chung and ShenLong to the storage room that Ha Lin had briefly stayed in. He thanked me many times. As I returned to my own room, I couldn't help but feel a heavy weight over me. LeeQin had accepted God in Nanjing. He was a devoted person. He handed out his own food to the homeless, and visited homes to help people fix things or to be an extra hand. Yet he had never been lazy at the convent either. Kuo Min Tang probably never even realized they had lost such a hard diligent worker.

I went to the head mistress. She looked at my sad face and said,

"It is truly unfortunate."

"Do you know what he's suffering from?"

"I heard it was a rare blood disease. I was told that you knew Mr. Chung and ShenLong. Please take care of them."

I nodded. From then on, the Chung father and son made their living in the storage room. I introduced Kyoo In and ShenLong, who were of similar ages. Kyoo In, although shy at first, opened his heart when ShenLong showed off his lucky rabbit's foot. ShenLong showed it off proudly, and Kyoo In, never having seen such a thing before, became excited. The two played for a long time before being tired and falling to nap next to each other. There were other friends at the orphanage, but the two became best friends and did everything together. Although he didn't want to be separated from his father at first, after becoming friends with Kyoo In, ShenLong began to sleep over in Kyoo In's room, and sometimes, Kyoo In also went to sleep at the storage room.

I kept a regular check on LeeQin's face, and would go get medicine from the hospital. When LeeQin wasn't feeling so horrible, he would come out to tend to the farm, water plants, and cleaned the yard, running errands that didn't take too much out of him. ShenLong got along well with the other children at the orphanage and grew strong. Although he didn't have a mother, he was bright and seemed to shine a kind of motherly love toward other members of the orphanage. Kyoo In, who was closest to him, also saw a fast recovery in health. He talked well, did not fear the night anymore, and even began to open his heart, showing normal emotions. I decided that the Chungs arriving in Chongqing was a positive turn of events after all.

Although the doctor in Nanjing had predicted he would only live for another two months, LeeQin managed to pass the two month mark. On a random day into his sixth month, he suddenly had a severe cough and chest pain, and eventually coughed out blood. He tried to hide it, but the child came to me crying in the middle of the night, saying his father was bleeding.

I quickly put my clothes on and ran to the storage room. He could barely breathe from the coughing up blood. I called for Connie, and she ran to the hospital and brought a doctor on a night shift. As I waited for the doctor, I held onto Mr. Chung's hand and prayed. As soon as the doctor and the nurse came, they put an oxygen mask on him and kicked us out of the room. 30 minutes later, the doctor came outside and said,

"Mr. Chung LeeQin just passed away. Today is April 17, 1945, and it is four forty AM," and asked the head mistress to do a last prayer for him. I cried. From my eyes and my heart, sadness continued to flow out. And yet, ShenLong never cried. He held my hands tightly. But he never shed a tear.

The head mistress gave the last prayer.

"From now on, Mr. Chung will no longer suffer in pain or disease; he rests in the Lord's home forever,"

We all said our goodbyes as we cried. At his funeral, many of the patrons gave his only son ShenLong warm glances and gave him tight hugs. He knew of his father's death, and although he shed tears, did not move from the spot until the end, saying good bye to his father. I hoped that he would no longer be suffering in pain or in loneliness, that he's joined his wife, looking down on his child. I looked up at the sky, standing there, looking for a while. ShenLong and Kyoo In held hands tightly. Kyoo In hadn't quite understood what was going on, but when he saw ShenLong's sadness, he also cried. As I looked down at those children, I hoped that they would not have any more sufferings. On our way home from burying Chung LeeQin, no one said anything, but we all gave ShenLong a loving hug once more.

Twenty Three

Chongqing, July 1945

I was on my way to my room after a full day at the orphanage. Due to the orphanage being overcapacity, we would all return, utterly exhausted. For most of us, dragging our tired bodies back to the dorm room was a usual day. As I crossed the front yard, someone came up to me, catching me by surprise. It was Sun-Soon. As she was a soldier in the Choson Liberation Army, she hadn't come often to visit. But suddenly, she'd appeared at my convent. She then calmly asked for some time. So I agreed, and told her to wait by the storage room. After telling her the location, she disappeared into the darkness.

I'd been the one in charge of keeping the storage room organized. Although LeeQin had done the work while living there the few months, once he passed away, I took over once more.

Either way, I thought this and that, as I cleaned off, prepared a light dinner, and headed back to the storage room. Once I entered the storage room, I could feel a presence. I tried to turn the light on, but Sun-Soon whispered,

"Don't turn that light on!"

Startled, I stopped my actions. She quietly whispered, "Is there anyone outside? Carefully close that door and come in."

I quietly closed the door behind me.

"What... what's going on?" I whispered back.

"Sister, I committed a sin today."

"What?"

She didn't hesitate. "I killed two men. They were Koreans... Koreans..."

I waited until she finished talking. I had nothing to say. To think she'd killed someone... to some extent, considering she was a soldier, killing was part of her job. And yet, wasn't she a kind hearted woman? Her confession though... was shocking.

"They were trying to sell information regarding Chinese American spies and Choson Liberation Army members' identities to the Japanese military. After meeting you, I was under orders to take care of this issue. And I succeeded. But they weren't alone. They're probably looking for me right now..."

"What should we do?! Shouldn't you leave Chongqing? Wait... not now. Perhaps once it calms down a little..."

I thought carefully.

"Did anyone see you get here?"

She shook her head.

"No one saw me. I'm sure. I don't know much about my partner though..."

Then she begged me for help.

I thought of the underground storage. There is an extension to the storage room underground. LeeQin had found it by chance, and had fixed it up. It was closed off in the past because it wasn't used. One day, he told me to come over, so I went down to see very old wines used in masses. Below the stairs were books on catholicism, handmade blankets, and other rare church items, which seemed to be at least a century old. There were items to the side, and a small empty space on the other side.

I took Sun-Soon by the hand and lifted a panel up from the corner of the storage room. We carefully made our way downstairs. Once I took her down to the empty space where two people could stretch their legs at, I turned the lamp on.

"If you go over there, you'll find a small door that you can crawl through. It's linked to the main basement and there is a small washroom, so you can take care of your business there as needed. Do it quietly. Always lock the door, and don't come out. There are some dried foods on the left corner, so eat that. There are some raisins and sweet potatoes and things…,"

Sun-Soon replied,

"Sister, I will never be able to you pay you back for this."

Her eyes teary. I gave her a small handshake before coming back up the stairs, closing the door, and putting the bit of straws over it once more.

I closed the storage room, and carefully returned to my dorm room.

After finishing off work, I stopped by the orphanage briefly, and walked to the dorm room. I was too exhausted in body and mind to do anything else. There were too many patients who needed dressing, that I had to run left and right. As I returned, someone awaited me at the gate.

It was the police. They explained the situation that had happened yesterday, and asked me whether I'd seen Sun-Soon Kim. Connie came over by me then to say,

"Last night? She was with me. Sister Marta is too busy to do anything else,"

Policeman replied,

"Is that true? That's quite strange. Last night, two Koreans were shot and killed. In an office in Chongqing. Someone saw a Korean woman go up to that office. Someone also saw a Korean woman run into this area. We found out that the Korean woman and the nun, Marta knew each other well, according to Hai Yun Tsen of the Kuo Min Tang."

I tried my best to stay stoic.

"Yes, I know Mr. Tsen. I also know the Korean woman. But I did not see her last night. So I have nothing to say,"

Police asked us,

"Is it all right if we look over the convent, then?"

We said that they could.

They looked all over the place before stopping in front of the storage room. I thought my heart would stop. But they glanced around the storage room, tapped a few sacks, before coming back out.

They thanked us, and said, "If you ever see or meet her, please let us know."

I said I would, and they left. As soon as they were no longer seen, Connie and I returned to the dorm room. I breathed deeply before falling on my blanket, and I explained everything to her. Connie replied,

"I knew you were particularly late last night. But it's fortunate... they didn't find Sun-Soon."

I also nodded, and we soon fell into deep sleep from exhaustion.

On August 15, 1945, The Japanese Empire surrendered. People on the streets cried, laughed, and hugged each other. I also hugged Connie, ShenLong, and Kyoo In and laughed. But my laughing face was stained with tears.

The long war was finally over. I lost my father and my youngest sibling. And a lot of people lost their lives. But Japan failed to make China kneel. I was proud on some end. I felt proud to be Chinese, even if the pain in my heart, our hearts, and my face would disappear.

Sun-Soon was not yet free, so she'd planned on escape. She told me she would like to leave when people were being emotional, one evening, when I brought her a meal.

"Is that okay?"

"This is enough. I don't want you to suffer any longer," Sun-Soon was rather stubborn about it.

I didn't know much, but I knew I couldn't break her stubbornness or determination. Were all Koreans like this...? I thought. Yoshihiro Saito was also stubborn and had tendencies to do what he wanted to do. He'd saved me on his decision, and he could kill Japanese and Chinese people alike. Were there a lot who did what they said they would... or did I just meet such people?

I asked carefully, "Why did you kill your own people?" to Sun-Soon.

"I'm not trying to seek forgiveness. But they are the enemy of all Koreans! One acted like an employment placer, but then defrauded people to join the battlefield... or such horrible places, and other person found Chinese and Korean resistance members and reported them to the Japanese. In return, he received money and prestige. I did what I needed to do as a member of the liberation army. I don't regret it. If I need to do it again, I would. I hope to worship with you at the mass comfortably, and under better circumstances. Of course, as a proud Korean!"

she said, confidently.

She left the sanctuary. I stood for a long time as the soldier disappeared from my sight. Morning was coming up above the convent roof.

I eventually decided to leave my past to the Lord and the Mother, and to live a life where I help others overcome their own pasts. Just because I had lowered myself, it didn't mean that I wasn't depressed sometimes. Some days, I simply couldn't control my psyche. Especially in the winter, when my virginity was robbed away, under the winter full moon, that especially cold night would come to haunt me, taking my sleep away. I worried that I would never forget it. Embedded in my cells like a bedrock was those nightmarish memories, that no matter how old I got, it would never dilute. I was tired from the heartaches beneath my nun gowns, but there wasn't much else I could do, so I tried to get closer to God, by laying down on the sanctuary floor.

With the loss of his father, ShenLong's face began to cloud over a little. He spent more time alone, and he would spend his time lying on the pillow his father used to use in the storage. As it was, that day, after sister Maria alerted the disappearance of ShenLong, we began to look for him. But when Kyoo In and I found ShenLong and brought him back to her, Maria took him, making a joke of how she wanted as much love as Marta received, that we all ended up laughing. As the child grew, I decided I wanted to do everything I could for the child. LeeQin saved my life. The way we'd met made me feel that we were fated to be. As he grew older, I wanted to give him love, and find him new parents who would provide for him. As a nun, it was impossible for me to give him all of the love. We were sponsoring other children to be adopted abroad and within, so I thought it was a completely reasonable possibility.

I still heard nothing from Ha Lin, who I thought would return once Japan surrendered, and there was still no news on Qu Lin. I just wanted any news and waited for them, whether from Enan or Chongqing.

At the end of September, Connie and I were walking by the Yangtze River in Chongqing. Unlike the River before, the Yangtze was clean, and the cool air making ripples in the water. The cool and slightly fishy river water seemed as if all the pain that had befallen on China had completely been washed away.

I was usually tied up at the orphanage or the hospital. Approximately ten minutes of walk away from the hospital by the riverside, where the willows grew, was a special place and time for me. We finished on time today, which was a rare occurrence. Due to the civil unrest of political ideas, the celebration was rather short. Since who we associated with could determine our life and death, we had to be careful with whom we'd associate with; it felt as if we were walking on thin ice. As the civil unrest deepened, people began to compare the Kuo Min Tang and its ugly reality to the regimented life of the Communists. Many people hadn't forgotten the abuse by the Kuo Min Tang.

As I walked with Connie, conversing about nothing important, when we met Doctor Yoon, who worked at the Kuo Min Tang affiliated hospital. He was from Choson. He worked at the hospital operated by the Kuo Min Tang, and did mostly surgeries. I learned that a lot of intelligentsias from Choson were gathering in Chongqing. Gu Kim in politics to Soon Hui Bang in media. Many famous Koreans cooperated with the Kuo Min Tang in their anti-Japan and anti-Communist movements. Doctor Yoon never sided with any political parties, and merely asserted that he was just a surgeon. He ran toward us, gasping for air. Caught by surprise, the news he brought was even more of a shock.

"Ha Lin Chao is dead. His name was on the casualty list. There was a battle between the Kuo Min Tang and the Communists in Jeinam, and it seems Ha Lin unfortunately passed away,"

We could say nothing. I couldn't walk anymore. I just fell to my feet. My tears wouldn't stop. I cried for my brother. I cried for my family. Father, Ha Lin, and Yul Lin were no longer in this world, and I still knew nothing about Qu Lin. Although stubborn, the fatherly kindness of Ha Lin would no longer be near us. On that day, below the bluest day in autumn, yet another piece of my sky flew away. I had to feel the pain of losing my family yet again. The Yangtze quietly absorbed all of my sobs and quietly floated away.

Ha Lin's personal belongings arrived in exactly a week. I never even got to see his corpse, but instead received the family photo and a worn out 100 Yuian bill. We took that to the head nun, and asked for the last prayer; for the safety of our family until the end, and for Ha Lin's return, who left for the battlefield to find his family and siblings, only to come back dead…

A few months passed. I heard nothing from Sun-Soon since she left the sanctuary, and I slowly recovered from the sadness of Ha Lin's death.

The new year came and went. On New Year's day, Chongqing's air was filled with smoke, the smell of burning fireworks, and hope as people lit their fireworks. These days, life wasn't too difficult or painful; not many Kuo Min Tang troops could be seen these days.

One cold winter morning, I found someone loitering about by the main gate. To be exact, it was ShenLong and Kyoo In that had found him. They yelled,

"Sister, there is someone outside!"

A slight anxiety washed over me at the sight of an unfamiliar man, but upon recognizing his uniform wasn't that of the Kuo Min Tang, was relieved to know there would be no abuse, and walked toward him.

And then my breath caught in my throat.

He asked in a deep voice,

"Excuse me, is there someone by the name of Sel Lin Chao here?"

I couldn't see his face. My heart stopped. Then it began to thump, twice, no, thrice the speed. Thump. Thump! Thump. Thump! The eardrums felt deafened. Heat rushed to my face. I blinked several time.

"…!" I held my breath. The tone of the voice ringing above my head was lower and slower than that of Ha Lin.

"Ah, I'm… her brother. I somehow learned that she's here… so I came to see her," he explained.

I slowly raised my head. And we stood there, in silence, as we stared at each other.

The face I saw was slightly older, with some lines on his scowl line. It was Qu Lin, who was only two years older than me. On the straight and thick inky left eyebrow was a knife scar. The nose seemed to have been broken once, and his lip was in a thin line. But his dark and clear eyes were the same as before. It was really Qu Lin. He was the first to open his mouth. His voice was shaking as well. My throat was closed up, and I couldn't say a thing.

"Really… Sel.. Lin? Sel Lin!!??" I merely nodded, as I didn't trust my voice. He hugged me tightly.

"You're alive! You're truly! Alive!"

I heard him say; I felt my head get wet, and my tears wet his shoulder.

And we stood like that for a long time.

Twenty Four

Chongqing, January 1946

The meeting with Qu Lin was a miracle. I told him everything that had happened until that moment. Of course, … the event of that night under the full moon in Fu Ji Mao was something I couldn't tell even my own brother. But he seemed to know everything. I still didn't trust myself to tell him, of course.

"To think you were taken back to Nanjing! To think you survived Nanjing! You must have been a truly lucky and blessed child, Sel Lin… no, sister Marta,"

He said, as he smiled.

"Aren't you the lucky one? I still remember the backs of those Japanese soldiers who ran after you… how did you manage to survive!?"

"Well…"

Hesitant for a moment, he answered.

"My fast reflex, and as you said, a bit of a blessing.

Then he whispered,

"There were a few Chinese Communist soldiers hidden there. They had seen the Chinese people get executed by the Japanese soldiers and were enraged. They were really patrol soldiers though. So they saw me running away from the Japanese soldiers. And…"

He cleared his throat, gave a cough, and finished.

"They saved my life. They then hid me. The Japanese never found me, and they went back. From then on… I did my part to protect this country."

My eyes widened. Qu Lin was fighting the Japanese on the other side as Ha Lin. And I quieted down. To think, was there a sadder story… Qu Lin looked at me and asked, "Is something wrong?" I shook my head, unwilling to ruin our brief moment of happiness with the stories of our dead siblings, thinking that our feelings were more important. He then asked me,

"Did you hear anything about Ha Lin or Yul Lin?"

I answered truthfully,

"Ha Lin passed away on the battlefield in September. You Lin… much long ago…"

I cleared my throat. My heart teared in two every time I thought of her. Qu Lin looked at me, his eyes dull. But he didn't cry, unlike me. But his fist got redder and redder.

"If I were… if I were just faster…!"

he wrapped his head in his palm. As I could feel his pain, I tried to breathe in the heavy atmosphere.

In less than ten years, the Chao family had less than half of us left. We sent them a silent moment, to them, who had wilted even before they could flower.

Qu Lin couldn't stay long. He explained he had much to do, and got up.

"Oh, and,"

he mentioned, so I looked back at his face.

"Perhaps… you may get a sister,"

I blinked.

"What?"

"I found someone I care for. I want to spend my life with her,"

I hugged him in a tight embrace. If any one of us had a chance at happiness, we must celebrate. I told him.

"Truly, congratulations. I congratulate you with all my heart. Please bring a sister."

He patted my back and confidently walked out of the main gate.

A few weeks later, a letter arrived for me. When I opened the enveloped, I found a train ticket to Wuhan. The letter simply said,

It's time to meet your sister.

On March 29, I took the train to Wuhan. A few hours later, I got off at the Wuhan train station.

There, Qu Lin and Sun-Soon were standing next to each other, waiting for me.

The two held hands as they said hello, and I was completely caught by surprise at seeing Sun-Soon here. Sun-Soon's eyes widened the same way when she recognized me.

At Sun-Soon's

"Sister Mart?"

I could say nothing. Qu Lin simply asked,

"What… do you two know each other?"

We nodded, and he gave a light chuckle, as if the whole situation was set up.

The three of us left the station and walked. As I looked, all I could say was,

"Just how…"

We walked into a nearby hotel. We sat in a restaurant corner, and my brother told me,

"Chongqing is still dangerous for Sun-Soon, … so I called you to Wuhan instead."

"How… no… how…" I couldn't finish the sentence. "How did the two of you meet?"

The two gave me an unnatural smile, as if troubled. They answered without looking at each other.

"Ah, it's a bit complicated,"

Sun-Soon said simply.

"Hm… to say, we met because of work,"

replied Qu Lin.

I couldn't believe it. In a land this big, how did the two people I knew meet each other! Was such coincidence possible!?

"At least… you could… tell me where you two met?"

I carefully asked, and Qu Lin answered.

"We met in Beijing. Then I came to Chongqing because of work. I then found out about you living here in Chongqing, so came to see you. I never thought you knew each other."

"So when you talked about brining a sister…"

"I'd already been seeing her,"

he finished the sentence.

"When did you meet!?"

"Last… autumn,"

Sun-Soon answered.

"And we…"

Sun-Soon held Qu Lin's hand and put it on the table.

"plan to marry tomorrow,"

I was speechless for a while. I didn't know what to say. I was too bewildered. Qu Lin seemed to misunderstand my silence, and said in a stern tone,

"We already have made the decision,"

Sun-Soon asked,

"Are you okay, sister?"

I didn't know how to explain this feeling, but I wanted to congratulate them with all my heart. They were both damaged people, lived a difficult life, yet were warriors who survived the whole ordeal.

I smiled. Then I covered my hands on their tightly held hands, and put my hands on them.

"Congratulations, Qu Lin, and my new sister. I'm sorry that all this poor nun can do is wish you happiness."

Sun-Soon smiled as she shed tears, and Qu Lin's face was a mix of shock, of smile and sadness, a difficult to explain expression.

"There's no way I'd be against this. I was just so bewildered. In this giant country, … to think that two people I care about the most met, fell in love, and now plan to marry… it feels so unreal,"

Qu Lin's face seemed comfortable.

That night, Sun-Soon and I slept in the same room, and the next day, they went to the government office and completed a simple ceremony.

I asked Sun-Soon,

"Can I ask you what you loved about Qu Lin?"

She answered.

"mm… height,… sharp eyes, … but something that makes me feel warm…, I guess? He was so different compared to all of the Chinese and Japanese people I'd met…"

Her answer was that of someone in love. And we talked all night.

Next to Beijing was the Great Wall, and the first gate to the Silk Road. Apparently a lot of people had rode on a camel, with new dreams and for new future, to the West. He told Sun-Soon that if she wanted, they could go to Republic of Korea from there. Sun-Soon loved him, and he loved Sun-Soon too. So they spent the time together while in Beijing.

After the ceremony, they took the train to Beijing, and I waved at them as they went further away.

I couldn't contain my joy; how surprised and happy would she be. As I thought about my family, who were no longer with us, I hoped for blessing of my new family member.

Two days later, as if planned, the Kuo Min Tang and the Communists began a civil war, and I couldn't help but be amazed at the Qu Lin and Sun-Soon's timing in getting married.

Twenty Five

Chongqing, March, 1950

The city was quiet. It was too quiet. There were only the old, children, and women. All of the men, and even some of the teenaged boys were all taken away by the Kuo Min Tang under the mandatory draft, and the city began to feel like a deflated balloon. The hospital, bank, and everything being closed, many people had to resort to bartering to make their living. The rest, being jobless, begged on the streets or would loiter around the roads. Head mistress tried to hand out some rice and vegetables, but was unable to do so due to the sheer number of need versus availability. And the situation was continued to worsen compared to four years ago. Everyone whispered every day that the Communists and Mao Tse Tung would come invade the city, and said powerlessly, that when the Communists and Mao arrived, they'd kill everyone in this city, especially since this was under the control of Kuo Min Tang. The convent held a gloomy mood as well. Last year, Mao said that the reason China had been the target of outside influences and suffered was because Western religion shook the foundation of Confucian belief system of China. He said he'd only recognize the Chinese Christians. Mao's decision to interfere with religion began to cause friction with the Roman Catholics, which impacted us at the end.

After Qu Lin and Sun-Soon got married, I couldn't see them again due to the war. On one hand, I worried. Sun-Soon had worked for the Kuo Min Tang as a nurse, but she was now living in the capital of the Communists. I really wanted to contact them. I was very worried about her.

One day, head mistress called me to her office. Then she told me,

"Sister Marta, I wish you'd study a little more and help the growing Chinese populous gain hope and attain a proper mindset. As you know, the government is now limiting our religion. So in the past, I've been asking for your study abroad.

I couldn't answer her, hesitating. She walked over to me and grabbed my hand.

"Come with me to the United States. We can worship the Lord and our Lady, and you can grow through knowledge," she convinced me.

"Thank you for your support for my study abroad,"

I bowed down, thanking her.

She smiled back at me.

"I also… felt the desire to restart studying, and it never went away, but…" she looked at me.

"I have too many things in China that aren't resolved. How could I leave my homeland like this?"

She thought quietly before she made a guess.

"If it's about ShenLong and Kyoo In, I understand. I already asked the headquarters about the boys, and received permission to bring them with us. I think their young age helped,"

I nearly jumped at her words. But I had to ask them. I couldn't make the decisions alone.

"I will ask the children, and get back to you."

"Sure! Do let me know as soon as you can,"

I gave her a light nod in response and left her office.

I ran toward the orphanage.

At age 13, Kyoo In and ShenLong were best friends. ShenLong was an adventurous mischievous boy. He had leadership and protected weak friends. Of course, he's sanguine temperament made him yell out things about justice especially when he saw something unfair. Compared to him, Kyoo In was a quiet and studious person. Unlike his childhood, he now could read and understand the meanings of sentences very well. But Kyoo In wasn't physically strong, nor did he get excited easily, and did not show his emotions easily. However, when they got together, no one could stop these two troublemakers. I found the two boys on their belly by the shade cackling.

When I called, "Kyoo In, ShenLong!" they raised their heads and got back up. They were still cackling. I thought that they'd done something. On their faces were mischievous and guilty looks.

"What did you guys do this time?"

I asked, and ShenLong answered,

"Sister, we're good kids. There's no evidence we did anything~," and smiled coyly. Wordless Kyoo In still said nothing, although his eyes seemed to sparkle he knew something I didn't.

I shook my head. Then I returned back to my state as a strict nun.

"Children… please listen carefully to what I'm about to tell you."

The cackling children saw my face and became serious.

"I will soon be heading to America."

Any smile remaining in their faces disappeared at this.

"A… America?"

Kyoo In managed first. His voice shook, as if he'd taken a huge shock. I nodded.

"Yes, America."

And then I sighed.

"So I was wondering, … since this decision is important to you, you must think carefully before making a decision."

The children looked, concentrating.

I took a deep breath. Then,

"Let's go together,"

I said to the children.

"What?"

asked ShenLong.

"China is still very dangerous, and Mao is coming from Beijing. Kuo Min Tang was also dangerous, … but the city they lived in, the convent, and we are also facing a great danger. It just happened that the head mistress asked the headquarters to let us go to America."

"So… does that mean we can all go together?"

Kyoo In asked.

"It seems so,"

I answered.

They looked at each other for a brief moment. Then they answered,

"We shall follow you, sister."

"Will you really not regret it? It'll be difficult when we first go to America. You have to study English, and adjust to the new culture? Will you be okay?"

ShenLong answered in a clear and powerful voice.

"Sister is like my mother. I'm sure I had a real mother, but the mother I remember is you, sister. If you're going, and if we're allowed to go, we're definitely going,"

Kyoo In nodded next to him.

"Wherever sister goes, as long as we're permitted, we'll follow." Finished Kyoo In.

As soon as the children said it, the heat that I kept inside my chest bursted out. I hugged both of them tightly, and said,

"Thank you, thank you so much. Thank you so much for saying you'd go with me. If you chose not to go, I wouldn't have gone either."

We told the head mistress our decision. But unlike before, her face was dark.

"Apparently, America is no longer accepting Chinese."

She answered. We were surprised at the completely different answer. ShenLong and Kyoo In stood, looked at the head mistress, their lips slightly protruding.

She told me,

"It's not quite set yet, … so let's look for another way."

And then she called me closer.

"Even if not America, we must leave China. Do not be lazy in preparation, and always be ready to leave,"

she whispered.

From then on, I began to organize everything. Most of the foreign nuns left the convent one by one, back to their native country. They had at first stubbornly refused to leave the convent for the sake of the children and the spiritual future of China, but the pressure from Beijing increased every day, so by the end, our convent only had a few numbers of Chinese nuns and a few orphans. Due to Kuo Min Tang's mandatory drafts the past four years, many boys were taken from the orphanage and did not return. Thankfully, Kyoo In and ShenLong, who were much too young at the time, and a few young boys were not forcefully drafted.

As the orphanage continued to quiet down, and the area near the convent also quieted down, Connie found me.

"Sister Marta! Head mistress is looking for you. Go to her room," and she left.

I went to her room.

"Thank you for waiting,"

The head mistress said to me, and handed me three train and ferry tickets. She then handed me a civilian clothing that seemed prepared, and said,

"This is a civilian clothing. Since the government and the Roman Catholics are in conflict with each other, do not act like a nun, and act as a civilian. I've registered the children as your sons. Here is your identification. Sons will be Chung Shenlong and Kyoo In Chung, who is one year younger according to the document. This is only applicable in China. You'll be able to get new identification once in Formosa. Please leave quietly as possible."

She crossed her chest and said, eyes teary, "The Lord bless you."

I bowed and thanked her deeply, and wiped the tears off of my eyes as I walked out.

That night, I quietly told Kyoo In and ShenLong to get ready. The next early morning at five, we took the train to go to Formosa. No one waved good-bye. I was very worried for Connie, but the head mistress said,

"Do not tell anyone that you're leaving for Formosa tomorrow," and since I wasn't the only one leaving, I couldn't say good bye either. Before leaving, I left a good bye letter in a location where Connie could find it.

Dear sister Connie,

I didn't realize the good bye would arrive so quickly. I couldn't say a thing. But to let you know, if we ever meet in Formosa, I hope to meet you again. Be healthy, and I hope the Lord always blesses you.

From Marta

I told the children not to call me sister. When Kyoo In asked,

"How do I call you then?"

I replied.

"Mother"

I told them their ages; Chung Shenlong, age 13; Kyoo In Chung, age 12. I told them to remember in case the customs officer asked.

I don't know how many hours had gone by. All day, my senses were on high alert. ShenLong was talking endlessly, and Kyoo In sat quietly on his first train ride. The air was excited, and my own nervousness made it difficult for me to rest the whole trip.

"Hey, Sis...!"

When ShenLong tried to call out, Kyoo In nudged him on the side hard. I hadn't heard him the first time due to being distracted by the area.

Kyoo In, who had sat between ShenLong and me, pulled on my sleeve as he said, "Mother!" and that's when I finally came to.

"How much longer, mother?" asked ShenLong.

I looked outside and saw that we hadn't yet arrived at Guiyang.

"We still have much left to go," I replied.

"But where are we going right now?"

Kyoo In asked quietly, and I contemplated an answer.

I had a strong inkling not to tell them the truth. They were still young. I patted both of them on the head and replied,

"We're going to the see the ocean,"

The place they nor I had ever been. We will see the ocean for the first time in our lives, and cross to go to Formosa. Their eyes widened, and began to get excited.

"Ocean!"

ShenLong and Kyoo In yelled at the same time, and we attracted the attention of everyone around us. I told them to quiet down with a "shhh!" and gave everyone a light bow.

Most of them went back to doing what they were doing, but the man in front of us seemed to look carefully at ShenLong and Kyoo In. I never let my guard at the way he looked at the boys. He didn't do anything suspicious. But I quietly held my guard until Hong Kong train station, as the voices of ShenLong and Kyoo In's conversations felt like music.

Three days after left Chongqing, we arrived at the sea shore that it was across from HongKong. HongKong was standing at close distance like reach out the continent to embrace. The sea was splendor view that we never expected. We planned to get one more voyage through the endlessness sea line. We are at the end of continent, the city of Yau Tong. We waited the ferry to get to HongKong. When we board at the ferry, the children's eyes were focusing to the totally different atmosphere, the wide opened sea.

HongKong, the city filled with hot humid air. Unlike Chongqing, HongKong was filled with foreigners in ostentatious clothing, and the eyes of the children widened at the sight.

Unlike the sleepy city of Chongqing, HongKong was filled with life. It was as if we'd arrived in a new country. In fact, HongKong was a different country. After the Opium War with the British, HongKong was part of our pride, given away. Quing Dynasty collapsed as a result of the war, and with it, brought the Sino-Japanese War to our front steps. Imperial Japanese took countless lives without any reason in China. For the past century, China has suffered much to bring back its identity, lost in the darkness. Isn't that why we're leaving China, heading to Taiwan? To give a better future to our children…

The children couldn't hide their excitement at the sight of the giant city. In order to focus their scattered minds, to get on the ferry, was wasting all of my energy. Once we visited a restaurant and bought steamed buns, the children calmed down and began to quiet down.

There was still some time left before ferry time, and we decided to eat dinner by the port area. It hadn't been a few hours since the steamed buns, yet hearing that we'd have dinner and take the ferry brightened their faces once more.

The children were busy looking at the port and people, and I held all of their luggage and held their hands tightly. I didn't want to lose the kids in this crowd. It was okay to lose the luggage. We walked around the loud Hong Kong port area, looking at this and that. For kids whose entire world was Chongqing, Hong Kong was a new world. Of course, it was the same for me. The kids who wanted to look around everywhere suddenly stopped. Their weight made me flinch.

When asked, "Why did you suddenly stop?"

"Si… mother…, over there!" Kyoo In pointed with his finger.

My eyes followed Kyoo In's finger. There was blue and wide ocean shining brightly under the sunlight.

Twenty Six

Riverside, November, 2014

And that was the end.

Hannah looked through the pages once more, but there were no more words nor pages to be found. Hannah's heart began to beat faster. Had she forgotten something… she thought to herself as she looked around once more, but she had read everything already.

She felt blinded. Did something happen afterwards? Why did it stop there? Hannah couldn't understand it. And she realized she wouldn't be able to find it there either. Hannah carefully organized everything in the pages. Then I put them all in an envelope, and put it in a safe in the master bedroom. Then Hannah began to think, before deciding she would need to meet with them. Summer's mother and father; she didn't know whether they would meet with her, but she had to try. Then she'd have to find them. Come to think of it, wasn't Summer's father also named Kyoo In? Could there be any chance of the story's Kyoo In being the same as Summer's father, Kyoo In? Such thought suddenly went through Hannah's mind. Anyway, Summer had risked her life to deliver these documents to Hannah, and she knew she'd have to find everything out or she simply could not survive.

To find answers, she opened up her Internet browser and searched for Kyoo In Wu. He was an East Asian history professor at UC-Berkely in California. Hannah immediately made a call to the school.

After the dial tone, a young woman's voice answered.

"East Asian History Department."

"Professor Kyoo In Wu, please."

"May I ask who you are?"

"My name is Hannah Walter. It is a personal matter."

"Please wait a moment, Ms. Walter."

A few moments later, Kyoo In Wu's deep low toned voice replied, "Ms. Hannah Walter?"

"Hello, professor Wu. How are you?"

"I'm okay. More importantly, I definitely didn't expect to hear your voice again. How can I help you?" He asked.

"Could you... meet with me?"

"But... don't you live on the East Coast?"

"Yes. But I plan to go to Berkely area in California tomorrow due to work. Do you have any time?"

"If that's the case, let's meet at the Darian restaurant in the food court of the campus. Is that all right? Have you been to the school campus before? If you enter the school, you can see the information sign, but you'll have to get a visitor pass sticker. How do you plan on coming? If it's taxi, it shouldn't be a problem. If you tell the taxi driver Darian restaurant at UC Berkley, they all know," He said.

"I'll do that. I'll meet you there," Hannah then hung up and began to look for a plane ticket to California. Then she booked a ticket to San Francisco evening plane, and packed simple clothes and toiletries in her day bag. She then put everything she'd translated deep inside her bag. Afterwards, she called Clint. It was currently three in the afternoon, and the plane was to leave at six. It was time to leave. He didn't pick up, and she left a simple voicemail, letting him know she was flying out to California to meet with Kyoo In Wu, Summer's father.

As she opened the door to the garage, she checked all of the windows and doors. Then she opened a secret door located behind the drawers in the garage, and turned on the security system. She turned the ignition of the car, brought the car out, and then closed the garage door using an automatic remote. As Hannah drove toward the airport, few minutes later, she began to notice a car in the back changing lanes every time she did. Hannah began to get nervous. Her chest began to pound loudly before she felt it stop. Her hands on the wheel shook slightly, and her palms felt damp.

Someone was trailing her!

Hannah's entire sense was focused on the front, back, and the sides, as she swerved in and out of the lanes and tried to lose the car behind her. When she moved left or right, she could see that car doing the same. She took the next exit. It was near Cafe Mundo. The car also followed me, taking the exit and continuing its pursuit of her. But due to the area having military bases, the rush hour traffic always started earlier than other areas. Hannah changed lanes in the slowing traffic, and was able to gain a more accurate observation of the follower: a black SUV.

"You've got to be kidding me; this isn't some sort of a movie! How could a car like that be following me?!"

Hannah looked at the back mirror once more. She squinted to make out the face of the driver, but he was wearing dark sunglasses. Nevertheless, it didn't feel comforting. She could see one of the hands being gloved.

Danger. Hannah gulped down air and looked straight. Then she changed lanes once more. Her cell phone rang on the side. It was Clint. She turned the speakerphone.

"Hello,"

"Hannah?! What do you mean, going to California!?"

Hannah realized her voice was calm, despite her trembling and damp hands. She tightened her grip on the steering wheel and made a quick turn to the right, and changed the lane once more. This time, the car couldn't catch up to her movement.

"Clint, there is even a greater problem."

"What's greater than you suddenly going to California?"

"Someone is following me."

"... What?"

"The license plate number is... Things may get dangerous. Wait, it's XGR...67...49. If anything happens to me, it's them."

"Wait... What!?"

"Also..." Hannah licked her lips. Her mouth felt dry.

"If anything happens to me, please take care of the file in the safe! I'm still driving... I'll call you when I get to the airport!"

"Wait... Hannah!"

Hannah hung up the phone, and paid complete attention on the pursuer and the driving. It became clear to her that she needed to lose the pursuer. She continued on the right lane a little longer before eyeing the exit.

That exit had a very short ramp, and was packed with cars, forming a slug like pace. Hannah slowly began to maneuver the car towards the exit. She looked at the rear view mirror and saw the pursuer do the same. She acted as if she were going to take the exit, and right before she entered the ramp, she swerved out and took the immediate exit back onto the highway. As Hannah looked back, she saw the driver panic as he was being blocked in by the other drivers behind him, and this led him down out of the highway.

The road Hannah swerved into was an unknown path frequented only by the neighborhood people. Since it was a backroad, Hannah was able to relax and drive.

Although the road taken took longer to get to the airport, she saw the shortened rays of the late autumn Sun through the leafless branches of the trees. Soon, she met the wider road leading to the airport, and on that road, she made a right turn.

Time was 4:30; Hannah hurriedly parked her car in the lot, and ran into the airport, cell phone and luggage in hand. Due to her frequent travels from the not too small nor big regional airport, the staff and crew were familiar with her. She showed the staff member Mark her bag and identification, and went into the gate. Thankfully, the man with the black leather glove was nowhere to be seen.

Before leaving for JFK International Airport, where she'd catch a plane to San Francisco, Hannah sent a text message to Clint; that she was safe…

She sat down and looked out. A few moments later, gate check completed, and the airplane door closed. Everyone put their seatbelt on, and the plane began to move toward the runway. The propeller began to spin. As the plane began to speed toward the end of the runway, I looked outside and felt my heart stop. A black SUV ran into the runway, speeding toward the airplane. At that moment, the plane began its ascent into the air. Hannah breathed a sigh of relief as she saw a black dot stop at the end of the runway.

Approximately an hour later, the small airplane with approximately fifteen or sixteen passengers arrived at JFK International Airport. Hannah entered the airport and turned the cell phone back on. There were ten missed calls and twenty texts from Clint waiting for her. Hannah called him.

"Hannah!?"

"I was sorry about that just now, Clint."

"What the hell is going on?"

"Someone was definitely chasing after me. Definitely… I think… I'm caught in something."

"I looked up that license plate; XGR-6749. It's a rental… just who is coming after…"

Then Clint suddenly stopped talking.

"What… why did you stop!? Clint? What's wrong?"

"I… I think I've seen this plate before. The time when our house was broken into…"

"N… No way!"

Hannah couldn't believe it.

"I don't quite remember… but there was a black SUV in my memory. I think that car also started with XGR. No one in our neighborhood drives around such a car."

That was true; although the neighborhood didn't lack money, no one drove around a car like that; since most were an older generation. Fear overtook her.

"Why are you suddenly going to California?"

"I plan to meet... Kyoo In Wu."

"Kyoo In Wu?"

"Summer's father."

"Why? Did you find something?"

Hannah shook her head, unaware that she'd done so.

"Be careful, and I'm also going to send this information to the police... where in California are you headed to?"

"Berkely."

"Be careful! Hannah, I don't know what it is, but your life isn't safe, especially considering the suspicious death of Summer.

"Uh-huh. I understand. Clint, you too..."

There was still about forty-five minutes until the San Francisco plane was to leave. As Hannah waited by the gate, she found a nearby hotel closest to UC-Berkeley, and reserved a room for two days. After she put her phone away, she glanced around her as secretively as she could. She became aware of the possibility of someone spying on her; and that she didn't know their identities. And yet, there was still not much she could do. Such feelings came with an accompanying feeling of powerlessness; the forty-five minutes she spent as she felt suffocated and anxious as she glanced around her for clues of the unknown spy.

She soon got on the plane, and she carefully thought out her plan of "attack," sitting curled up for the seven hours of flight. What she would ask Kyoo In Wu, what he would know, and whether he would be able to relieve some of this curiosity, and whether he'd be truthful in their conversations; she was curious about it all.

The plane continued to fly to its destination like a bird, its wings wide, on the sky as blue as the sea. As the plane flew further from the ground, the blinding sunlight in the sky forced Hannah to close the shade.

When had she fallen asleep? Hannah got up, rubbing her eyes. When she looked at the small screen on the headrest in the front, and realized they'd just entered California. ETA 30 minutes; Hannah stretched her arms and moved around to free her cramped muscles. Time of truth was coming closer, step by step.

Once she got off of the plane and took the taxi into the hotel, it was already ten at night. Hannah unpacked and opened the curtain. The quiet Berkeley evening welcomed Hannah. She took out the organized pack of papers, and looked them through once more. Events of the day like today had completely disorganized her head. But She'd arrived safe. All of her documents were safe. Hannah texted Clint:

"I've arrived at the hotel safely. Don't worry,"

She could see that he was also writing something to her. He must have been wondering about her arriving safely, and wasn't sleeping.

"Thanks! Hannah, I can sleep now. Thanks. Good night! I'll also sleep now," she read.

Hannah took a shower and lied on the bed. Sleep did not come; her head felt so clear. She tried to sleep. And she decided she needed to stop thinking, so she checked the hotel door one more time, and pulled the duvet all the way up to her head and closed her eyes. As she slept, she dreamt. She saw the Yangtze River. The bloody waters of the Yangtze sloshed before wriggling and turning into a shape. Bloody water started to get up and began to walk. The shape was an animal with many legs, with a shape of the dragon. It seemed to be burning with fire, and it seemed to have a mouthful of fire; the dragon was moving against the current of the river. It slowly came closer to Hannah. Surprised, Hannah nearly fell out of the bed, and opened her eyes. Thankfully, it was just a dream. The clock next to the bed blinked 12:00 PM.

With a gasp, she jumped up. Hannah glanced about, before rushing into the bathroom. She quickly took a shower, brushed her teeth, and towel dried her hair; it was 12:20. Hannah then put her clothes on, took her handbag with bunches of paper, and took the hotel keycard before rushing out of the hotel. She caught a taxi and barely managed to arrive at the restaurant, and looked around.

Kyoo In Wu was sitting by the windows. Unlike before, he looked like a stereotypical professor, in a tweed jacket, brown color sweater, and corduroy pants. Like before, his face showed just a shade of darkness. Hannah brushed her damp bangs and walked towards him. Once she got closer, Kyoo In Wu got up off of his chair. He gave a simple bow, and pulled the chair opposite him for Hannah to sit on.

"It's been a while, Ms. Walter."

"How have you been?"

"Could be better. Anyway, my students recommended this place to me. The food's not bad."

"Ah, I see."

"You've come from a very far place. By the way, what brings you to California?"

As she met his honest eyes, Hannah took a sip of water and cleared her throat.

"Do you... know or know of a nun named Marta, or of Sel Lin Chao?"

As soon as he heard her name, his facial expressions changed immediately.

"What... I mean... so suddenly...?"

"Actually... Summer left me something. It was Sel Lin Chao's diary. I put the diary in a safe place... but... these are the documents I translated since then."

His entire body shuddered, as his shaky hands received the bunch of papers. Hannah continued, as she observed his reactions.

"Do you... know her?"

Kyoo In took his eyes off of the papers and looked at Hannah. They stared at each other in silence for a moment. After what seemed like an eternity, Kyoo In opened his mouth.

"She was like my mother."

"So the Kyoo In in her diary was you after all."

"Probably."

"To be honest, I came to see you today."

"You came to California to see me?"

"That is correct." Hannah nodded.

Another moment of silence floated by like the waters of a river. Kyoo In began to speak again.

"What is it that you want from me?"

"I want to know the ending of this story."

"Sorry?"

"I want to know what happened after you all arrived in Hong Kong. What happened afterwards, and how you ended up in America... I want to know it."

"Is it that important to you?"

"Yes."

"I'm actually being followed," when Hannah admitted, Kyoo In's face began to freeze.

"They followed me all the way to the airport. Although I managed to lose them and get to the airport and even here, safely."

"That's quite serious..." the shadows on his face got darker. He seemed to age at least ten years in the short time we were sitting there.

"Sorry? What do you mean?"

"Summer... also met people like that," said Doctor Wu.

"What!?"

Hanna was surprised.

They were dangerous after all.

"Before Summer died, she began to take an interest in her real parents."

"Sorry... real? Summer's not your biological parents?"

"No. I adopted her. And at the time, I thought it was about time that she knew. There was no point in hiding it at that point, when she knew. It was difficult for me to reveal her roots, but she wanted to know and I was obligated. To think that would drag her to death..." he gripped his hands tight.

"I really didn't know."

A horrible excitement rose in Hannah. Who were they, truly? Those pursuers and Summer's death could be related. But Hannah tried to maintain calm in a swirl of emotions.

"As long as I have these documents from Summer, I can't stop."

As he stared into her determined eyes, Kyoo In replied,

"There isn't much else I can tell you. Just like that… we went to Taiwan, and lived at the convent there. Then… we came to the United States. I was accepted for undergraduate studies at Stanford University, and sister Marta went to the East for an assignment, and graduated from the Catholic University there."

We took another sip of tea as we waited for food. Kyoo In continued.

"My friend chose not to leave Taiwan. He wanted to protect Taiwan, so did not come to the States. He said he'd work for China, close from where his parents were buried. Sister also returned to Taiwan after finishing her coursework. And ShenLong, he was the father of… Summer."

"Ah…" Hannah unknowingly let out a sigh. The sadness for Summer's death and her knowledge of her parents' fate… how lonely did she feel…? Such thoughts weighed down on her heart.

"I found out that my friend and his wife passed away from an accident, so I decided to bring Summer to the United States, and to raise her. She was five. So naturally, she wanted to know about her parents as she grew up. I was just trying to help her."

His voice began to shake harder and harder.

Hannah told him that she'd plan to visit China. Dr. Wu then wrote down for her the recent address of Sun-Soon Kim, and that he'd call his colleague, Le-Xin Hui, professor at Jin Ling University, and handed her the email address and phone number of Jin Ling University.

Hannah could understand how difficult of a life Dr. Wu had. How had he lived through such a life? He lost his parents and friends through war, and finally, lost his child. How many people were living with the weight of war, always being reminded of the pain and torture from the memories of the past? Hannah's mind and heart filled with pain.

Hannah and Kyoo In spent a longer time, and she was able to question him and fill out the holes in her mind, especially of the time spent in Taiwan. Hannah couldn't solve all of her curiosity, however. Sel Lin Chao was surprisingly a quiet non-talkative person. Hannah bid Kyoo In good bye after lunch, and walked out of the UC Berkeley campus to head back home, but saw a black car parked across from the restaurant. Hannah unconsciously jumped. She clearly felt a trauma of black cars; but then she stopped on the spot. A man wearing black gloves sat, tightly holding onto the steering wheel. He had on black sunglasses. He didn't seem like the man Hannah had seen yesterday though. He was much younger. Hannah wondered if he'd seen her or not. If he'd seen her, he could pursue her. So Hannah walked around to the back, and walked out the other exit. She then got on the taxi and decided that it'd be safer at home. She remembered that she hadn't checked out of the hotel, and that her luggage was still at hotel. She decided to check out at the hotel and get her luggage, and asked the taxi driver to take her to the hotel. He drove over to the hotel. But once she arrived, she saw yet another black sedan by the hotel entrance. Without getting out of the taxi, she asked the driver to drive to the airport instead. He of course did as he was told.

Once they arrived, Hannah gave him an additional tip of $100, which made the driver thank her profusely. Hannah bought the earliest flight ticket and headed to the gate. Even on her way home, she never felt comfortable, and looked around anxious. The returning flight itself wasn't too comfortable either.

She contacted Clint, and he promised to come out to meet her. She could feel herself getting tired.

How did they know she was taking the flight to Berkeley? What did they want from her, and why were they pursuing her? Also… are they responsible for Summer Wu's death? If that's true, why did they kill her?

By the time she'd arrived back at the home airport, the Sun had set, and it was quite dark. She spotted Clint almost immediately. He waved at her lightly and came over to her.

"What… you only took a handbag across the country?"

Hannah shook her head.

"No… but… I couldn't bring back my travel luggage."

"What… again?"

"To be honest, I don't know if those people were them, … but… I just… I was too scared to go back into the hotel."

"That was a good decision."

"There were only pajamas, an outfit, and underwear."

"Okay, that's a relief."

Clint gave Hannah a tight hug. She also embraced him, her arms tightly around his waist, and rested her head on his shoulders. She didn't know how long they'd been standing like that. Hannah told Clint she'd parked on this lot, and they walked toward where she'd parked. But no matter how many times they circled around, they couldn't find her car. She felt the hairs on her back stand up. Clint also scowled, as he looked around looking. After what seemed like hours, they went over to the airport security and reported a missing car. They said they'd ask around and let us know the next day. Hannah got in Clint's car without a word. Hannah's dark house seemed to prove the effect of her one day absence. She first turned on the light in every room of her house, walked to the kitchen, and ate a simple dinner. Just where was Hannah's car?

Hannah first called up the hotel, told them due to a sudden event, she couldn't check out nor could she take the luggage. The hotel manager then hung up. After she took care of the hotel check out issue and the luggage issue, she took a shower and lied on the bed. For the first time in a long time, she was on the bed staring at Clint.

Hannah talked first. She then explained all of the things that happened, to Clint, including her meeting with Professor Wu, and the secret behind Summer's birth.

"So…" Hannah suddenly grabbed Clint's hand tightly.

"Clint."

"What?"

Clint answered, wary.

"Let's go to China!"

She exclaimed.

"China?"

"The answer is… in China. The beginning and the end of this story… it's China. Probably… if I got to China, I could find all of the answers to this."

Clint gave her head a light pat, sighed, and reciprocated the grabbing of hands.

"Okay. I guess you're the one that needs to finish this story. That's the answer to the friendship you have with Summer. Why she died, and how related to this situation everything is. You've been vigilant about solving this, risking your life. So we should probably end this on a good note, so all that you've done doesn't end in vain. That's also the right thing to do…"

Clint then held Hanna tightly, and the two slept a comfortable and deep sleep for the first time in a long time.

Twenty Seven

Riverside, March 2015

In the end, no one could figure out who took Hannah's car. In the security camera, it showed two men get out of the black sedan, walk to Hannah's car, where they stuffed something into the window, opened the car door, and drove her car out of the parking lot, but the resolution was too low for them to get a clear view of the faces. They had on hats and dark sunglasses.

Detective Jameson took this case as well.

"You are having one unlucky year," he said, his face showing a complicated expression.

Eventually, Hannah's car was found in a ditch, on a dead end, near the airport. Nothing was stolen. But the car was in disarray if someone was trying to find it.

Hanna decided not to trust anything eventually. She was in so many dangers. However, she can't ignore that kind of dangerous situations any longer either. The most urgent business, she has to find out of the connections between the Summer's story and the end of Sel Lin Chao's.

"So did you get all of the information you could have gotten from Mr. Wu?" Clint asked, packing the luggage even more compact.

Hannah nodded.

"Yes. And I've already called the Catholic University in Washington, D.C., and Dr. Wu also introduced me to Le-Xin Hui of Jin Ling University, so I've already emailed him of our arrival."

Clint then pulled the luggage and said, "Shall we head out, my lady?" and gave her a grin. He turned the security system on. Hannah carefully packed Summer's documents in an envelope and placed it deep in her purse. She also put the translated documents deep in her carry-on case.

They locked the door and got into Clint's car inside the garage. Then Clint drove the car to the Riverside Regional Airport.

They then arrived at the international airport. Hannah and Clint walked toward their gate, to their plane headed for Shanghai. They had a steak and salad for lunch.

A little after two in the afternoon, Hannah and Clint got on the plane for Shanghai. They sat in the business class seats, as Clint had paid the extra money for it. They sat by the windows, and put the carry on in the above space. They then sat comfortably in the wide seats.

As they were busy trying to get on the plane, they never noticed the man in black suit and leather gloves sitting behind them.

Once everyone got on the plane, the plane began to speed up on the runway. With the feeling of the body floating, and the ears becoming stuffed, the Plane began its ascent towards Shanghai.

Le-Xin Hui was waiting at the Shanghai airport. He was much taller in person, and it was easy to see that the photo he sent over email didn't do him justice. He looked more alive and was a gracefully aging professor. He was a women's history professor at Jin Ling Women's University. He seemed to be of similar age as Kyoo In Wu. His head was completely white, but his eyes seemed bright, clear, and constrained.

"Mrs. Hannah Walter, right? You came a long way," Professor Hui extended his hand and shook Hannah's hand.

"Nice to meet you, Dr. Hui. Thank you for coming out to meet us. This is my husband, Clint Walter," Hannah introduced her husband to Dr. Hui.

"Hello, Dr. Hui. I'm Clint. Nice to meet you. The weather here is much warmer than in the States," Clint exchanged light pleasantries with Prof. Hui, and the two exchanged a hand shake as well.

"Shall we first head to the Nanjing? Since you said you were being followed, I've been thinking a lot about this. Let's talk on the way. The car is parked outside," said Prof. Hui as he began to make his way to the airport exit.

The warmth on the parking lot in Shanghai made her realize spring had arrived. People were in light clothes as well. Hannah took off her coat and put it in her bag. Clint also took off his jacket and hung it over his arm. He then pulled the luggages with him as he followed Prof. Hui. The couple got in Prof. Hui's car, and Prof. Hui began to drive towards Nanjing, leaving the airport. After a while, they began to see high rise buildings. Prof. Hui explained that it was Shanghai's pride and joy, the 101 floor skyscraper. It was completed in 2013, and people could see the expanse of land that was China in a glance. The Hyatt hotel was between floors seventy nine to ninety three, and explained that every Chinese person wanted the opportunity to have a meal and shop there for a birthday present, at least once. Shanghai was gigantic, reminiscent of the giant port city of the past. From the port to the airport, and into the city, as they drove, the city that was completely destroyed because of Japan's invasion was long gone, organized, filled with energy. She suddenly saw New York City back in the States.

Clint sat in the front, and Hannah sat in the back. Prof. Hui drove, and explained that he didn't have much memory regarding the Nanking Massacre, but knew much about it. Hannah could tell his dedication to education at Jin Ling. He asked Hannah,

"You do realize how difficult this is, right?"

"Yes, at first I didn't. But now that Summer Wu passed away, with the diary she handed down to me, I was able to see Sel Lin Chao's life, about Nanjing, and even of the people following me, which is all chaotic. That's why Clint accompanied me this time," His eyes seen through the back mirror seemed understanding.

"Prof. Wu said you wanted to visit Fu Ji Mao, and to help you with safety there. Is there a special reason for why you want to visit the place?"

"More than a special reason, It's the place that linked Summer Wu, Sel Lin Chao, and me to Nanking Massacre."

"Well, if you need my help, always call me on my number. Of course, since your husband is with you, I don't think I need to worry. Did you book the hotel I introduced? It's near Qin-We river, by Fu Ji Mao," finished Prof. Hui; then suddenly he stepped on the brakes.

At the sudden movement, Hannah's body bolted forward then back. It was a good thing that she'd put on the seatbelt. Prof. Hui and Hannah's bodies both shook severely.

"A strange car kept following me from the airport. I didn't think much of it, but we've been on the same road for the past two hours. I've been watching, continuing to talk to keep from being too nervous. But suddenly, the car sped right behind me. I slammed the breaks to startle him, but I wasn't able to see his face. He's wearing sunglasses and black gloves, but doesn't seem to be Chinese," finished Prof. Hui.

Hannah felt her heart stop. As soon as she turned around to verify the identity of the pursuer, the car changed lanes and sped off.

"There was a man pursuing me when I went to meet Dr. Wu as well. He also was in a hat, sunglasses, and black gloves," replied Hannah.

"That's right, you told me about someone like that following you. Do you think they possibly followed you here?" asked Clint.

Dr. Hui's eyes widened in surprise.

"He was so strange. He kept up speed with me the whole time. He could have passed me, but he didn't. Then suddenly, when I finally stepped on my brakes, he choosed to move away to another lane. Do you think he changed the lane and left because he thought we got suspicious?

"It's certainly a possibility," replied Clint.

On the way to Nanjing, he drove past Zhenjiang as Hannah had wanted. Although he was a 78 year old man, his senses and reflex were comparable to those of the younger generation. Hannah thought that perhaps his job as a professor, and being surrounded by the younger students probably kept him younger, for both Prof. Wu and Prof. Hui. That could be it. Really…

Zhenjiang was smaller than Shanghai. Zhenjiang was Sel Lin Chao's place of longing. It was her home city. Leaving Zhenjiang and going to Nanjing, Hannah was for a moment, Sel Lin Chao. Whether before or now, she didn't know how long it'd take to get to Nanjing.

The purple sunset covered a purple mountain by the time they arrived in Nanjing. As soon as they stopped at Hotel Regalia, they first checked in, and visited the hotel restaurant. The couple asked the professor to stay for dinner and to allow them to treat him; after all, he'd drove them all the way from the Shanghai airport, and guided them safely to their destination. The hotel was enormous. There was a mood to it unfelt in America. On the table was a purple silk table cover with flower decorations, and through the windows, the view of Qin We river mixed perfectly with the Sunset. The restaurant's menu was diverse, from Chinese, Japanese, and various meat dishes like steak and lobster. Clint and Prof. Hui ordered the steak, and Hannah ordered the lobster. Clint ordered red wine, but Prof. Hui declined, stating he had to drive back home. As his house wasn't too far from Qin We river, he always recommended this hotel to his colleagues and friends from abroad. Before he left, Prof. Hui handed her a pistol inside a brown envelope. Since she couldn't bring it from the States, she'd asked for its preparation. She hoped she'd not have to use it, but after seeing Summer's death, Prof. Wu had requested it from Prof. Hui. A pink Electra handgun was sitting inside it.

Under the Communist regime, unauthorized gun possession is illegal. However, as Doctor Hui was part of a hunting group and held a hunting license, he had limited access to guns. However, to avoid detection, there must have been some sort of a black market deal; as the pink Electra pistol isn't a gun typically used in hunting. Hannah hid the gun deep within her purse.

In fact, Hannah learned how to use the pistol at indoor shooting ranges when she was in her 20s. After she lost her parents, she was wallowing in deep despair and desperation. She wanted to escape from the loneliness of losing both her siblings to their respective marriages and wanted to escape the depression, and decided to learn to protect herself. After school, she would practice shooting at the range before returning to the school library, stooping over her table to complete her research papers. It was there, on one fateful day, that she met Clint.

After dinner, they walked Prof. Hui out to the hotel lobby. Hannah and Clint walked to the elevator to get to their room, 773. They then pressed the button for the 7th floor. Most of the people in the elevator were either travelers or Chinese people. As soon as they got off, they headed straight for their room; Hannah wanted to fall straight onto bed, but chose to take a shower first. The bathroom was large, just like China; it was much more elegant than a standard hotel in the States.

Clint opened the window. The sky was turning from purple to dark blue, where even the clouds quieted down, and the night continued to deepen. As Clint looked at the lights of Nanjing, he saw the endless beams of light from cars, and the colorful lights from endless rows of restaurants; the China of now shone in Clint's eyes.

Summer's death changed Hannah completely. Before she met Summer, Hannah existed as Clint's wife, and the mother to their children, a housewife dealing with menopause. But after meeting Summer, life seemed to come back to her. With Summer's death, Hannah seemed to be sucked in darkness. That was his impression of his wife, Hannah. But as he stared at the lights in the dark Chinese sky, Hannah would have to realize how strong a human being must become through death of Summer, the sadness and unresolved sorrow of the Yangtze; it was good that they came to China. As Clint thought endlessly, Hannah walked up behind him.

"It's your turn, Clint. I'm done," she said. He could see steam coming off of her body, and her face and eyes were red from tiredness.

"Yes, of course. I must also shower... it was a tiring day," he said, and closed the curtain back up before heading to the bathroom.

A few moments later, Hannah changed into pajamas and lied on the bed. Everything on the bed was purple with a small strip of line going through, whether it was bed sheet, duvet, or the pillow. Hannah thought that it was due to the close proximity to the Purple Mountain.

She wrote down all she planned to do the next day in her notebook. She would visit Fu Ji Mao to see if she could find the item that was hidden; What was hidden, why did Yoshihiro leave that in China? What did it mean to Sel Lin Chao? Such thoughts, of opening the secret in just a few hours, made her excited.

Once Clint finished showering, he came out and pulled out wine from the refrigerator. He poured two cups; they finished the wine and lied down on the bed.

She had a dream. Hannah was walking on the river bank, and the harsh red sunlight burnt up all of the rotting fish, which were floating up the river. Hannah covered her nose, as the smell of burning fish made her feel sick. She was alone. The red Sun began to run toward her. Hannah wanted to escape, but found her legs unmoving. She screamed, and as if startled, the Sun stopped moving. She began to run then. She didn't know how long she'd sprinted, but when she turned around, she heard music playing. There were much tears in the sad, mourning music. As Hannah turned around to walk forward, she saw a woman standing in front of her. She indicated two dragons were engraved at the wall. She held Hannah's hands. They were warm. They felt rough like Hannah's mom's, but very warm. She hugged Hannah tightly. When Hannah looked back at her, it was Summer Wu. Surprised, she called out Summer's name, and was abruptly awoken.

Clint was still next to her, sleeping deeply. Hannah realized how strange the dream was. For the first time since the death of Summer, she saw her, alive, in her dream. The fact that she was warm rather than cold made her feel as if she was in a complicated quiz.

Hannah and Clint washed up as soon as they awoke in the morning, and headed to the hotel restaurant. It was for breakfast before the day's full schedule. The plan was to check out Fu Ji Mao first. Sel Lin's diary mentioned a location where the moonlight shone diagonally. And to see where the moonlight hit, they'd have be come back at night, but it was important to see where everything was.

Hannah and Clint had a simple breakfast, and left the hotel with simple gears. Of course, Hannah placed Sel Lin Chao's diary in her bag. When considering the things that had happened to her these days, someone wanted something from her. It made her question what that would be. Clint said that the hotel would be safe, and to leave without too many things, but Hannah said that it was safer to leave with them, and gave the her bag a small pat.

The road from the hotel to Fu Ji Mao as they glanced at the Purple Mountain wasn't too far. Prof. Hui's recommendation was truly helpful. In front of the Fu Ji Mao's great sanctuary was the statue of Confucius.

Twenty Eight

Standing on the path to the main sanctum, were the statues of Confucius's pupils, facing each other. On the top of the steps, Confucius stood with an awe-inspiring look. They went into the main sanctum. Confucius' altar was magnificently decorated.

Fragrant candles were burning in contained jars.

They looked around the inside of the main sanctum briefly before coming outside. Hannah could feel a headache coming on. How would they find this secret entrance connecting to the main sanctum? There was no indication or evidence of this door. They couldn't find the location written in Sel Lin's diary.

Her diary had described a wall that wasn't burned down or destroyed, located at the end of the left wall, but it was nearly impossible to distinguish which side hadn't been destroyed. The Chinese government had of course, completely renovated the place after the war.

Hannah try to think like Sel Lin, and decided to find where she could have seen this location, the place where the main sanctum, the stairs, and the left building could meet. Suddenly a thought came across. She thought about Summer pointing toward a dragon. The wall with a picture of a dragon, and the end of that wall…

After a little while, Hannah began to walk, and Clint followed her without a word.

Hannah thought about the right side of the left building, and the stairs. Once she got closer, she could see an area where the new materials connected to slightly older looking materials. She neared and carefully pressed on the corner. Her eyes widened. Clint couldn't say a word, dumbfounded. He looked around the area for her, and saw that they were the only people there. The door opened. Hannah wordlessly closed the door.

Hannah marked under the corner of the wall.

"Hannah, do you want to go out for some fresh air?"

"Should we? I sort of want to check out the back yard as ell."

"Yes, let's look around and come back once the Sun goes down," Clint whispered to Hannah.

As Hannah and Clint walked across the yard of the main sanctum, they saw another Chinese couple walk into the sanctum.

"Hannah, they didn't see us when we open the door, did they?"

"No way. How could they know?"

"You're right, how could they."

"Truly. Considering the diagonal line where the moonlight hits, I think I should try to guess where it is."

Hannah and Clint looked around the main sanctum, the smaller sanctums, and other sanctums and realized Sel Lin's descriptions were rather accurate. Although much time had passed, the Chinese government was trying to restore many, if not all of the cultural or historic sites.

The two walked out. As they looked at the restaurants surrounding the Qin We River, they couldn't help but be reminded of restaurants on the entrance to Richmond Island bridge in Riverside Community.

River is life. River is the lifeline to life. So maybe the restaurants opened up by rivers to stay alive, whetting their and others' throats.

They went into a restaurant. They sold various steamed dumplings. A steamy dumpling the size of a palm was the best dumpling they'd ever had. Hannah had lived with the thought that the dumpling her father made was the best in the world.

When she had the dumpling, she couldn't help but think of her parents. The kind father and the strict mother was Hannah's entire world. After losing them to death, she stopped eating dumplings because she kept thinking of her father. When one day, she met Clint, and became pregnant with their first child, she told him that she craved dumplings badly. Clint looked up the recipe, but it turned out to be a steamed bun rather than dumplings; she enjoyed it nevertheless. It wasn't comparable to her father's, of course.

"You seem to really enjoy this."

"It's delicious. It tastes like my father's dumpling."

"Didn't I make you one?"

"You did, but it was more of a bun than dumpling," Hannah said, grinning.

"If there's anything you want to eat, I'll buy it for you, so tell me if you want anything. I'll get it for you, of course, because you know my limits."

"Of course. Thanks. I'll remember that."

"Let's go look around a little more, and get something else if we get hungry."

"Should we?"

"We haven't had a trip between us for a very long time."

"Time truly has passed."

"All that time, I worked outside and you raised the children, did the housework, and lived industriously, and looked after me. That's why we have today. Thanks, Hannah!"

"I thank you too, Clint!"

Two of them walked arm in arm, for the first time in a long time, by the Qin We River.

Once the Sun began to set, Hannah and Clint returned to Fu Ji Mao's main sanctum. The sunset on the Purple Mountain was sitting on Confucius' head. As they saw the stairs, they thought of Sel Lin Chao. At the place where her pain was permanently etched, Hannah stood for the briefest moment.

Hannah and Clint went toward to the secret door where Hannah had marked earlier.

They pushed it. When the door opened, Clint took his cell phone and used it to shine on the area. There was a maze and they went to the secret maze. There were stairs. Sel Lin Chao's description was exact. Just as she'd explained, the area looked the same. There were spider webs everywhere, and spiders could be seen moving about in their own world, free. Once they came down the stairs, they were able to see the area where Sel Lin and Yoshihiro would have stared at each other and lied down on. Hannah told Clint to find the window, and there, they located a palm sized window. Clint pointed towards Hannah. From there, they located a diagonal location. But it was difficult finding a gap in otherwise perfectly symmetrical brick wall.

Clint looked around, before putting his hand on Hannah's head.

He pulled on one of the hairpins off of Hannah's head, and began to press on the wall with it, looking everywhere. Eventually, his eyes widened, and he stopped in a location. He handed the cell phone to Hannah.

"It's here! Shine the light here!"

"What, really? Okay!" Hannah then shone the cell phone there.

The brick piece moved. Clint carefully took the brick piece out.

There, she saw exactly four bricks out of the wall. Inside was a safe.

"What did you say the number was? Open the notebook. You wrote the number down."

"Give me a moment," Hannah said, as she handed the cell phone to Clint; she then pulled the notebook out of the purse and called the number out to Clint.

"3, 4, 23, 22."

"It's not working."

"Okay… try 22, 23, 4, 3."

"That doesn't work either!"

"Then do left 3, right 4, left 23, and then right 22," and Clint did as told. Once complete, they heard a click, and opened the safe door.

There was a notebook, red foot binder with a golden dragon drawn on it, some sort of a bead or marble wrapped in black fabric, and memo from Yoshihiro. Once they unwrapped the cloth, the items shone against the flashlight, and the inside became bright. Sel Lin's description was accurate. None of it was touched, like a treasure island... Clint turned the lighter off, and looked into it carefully. It was laminated by itself. It looked special.

They put the wall back into its original form, and checked to make sure everything looked as it did.

Hannah and Clint carefully wrapped the bead in the black fabric, put it in Hannah's handbag, and closed the zipper. Hannah took out the pistol from her purse and transferred it onto her jacket. Since the situation around Hannah was abnormal these days, Clint had told her to do so. They looked inside before making up the stairs. Sel Lin's pain in the past seemed to follow them. Perhaps the hidden truth was finally leaving this place, and into the world with Hannah.

When they opened the door up the steps, they could feel an unseen movement. Clint held onto Hannah's hands as they walked towards the entrance. Once they neared the end of the yard of the Fuzimiao, two masked men ran at Hannah and Clint. One of them pushed Hannah to the ground and grabbed at her handbag, and Clint retrieved it, putting the bag around his neck, and pushed Hannah to one side.

"Call Prof. Hui!"

"How? In this situation!?"

Hannah pulled her phone from her pants pocket and dialed the number.

"Dr. Hui, we're in danger at Fu Ji Mao...!" Before she could hang up, she saw Clint block their attacks, with the bag still around his neck.

Clint moved fast against the two men, occasionally kicking their sides or at their heads. Clint was in the special forces when he was younger, so he was trained. But the two men were also not easy to overcome. Suddenly, one of the men grabbed Clint from the bag. One of Clint's arm held the bag, although the other kept hitting him; Hannah pulled the pistol from her jacket at this moment.

She shot twice. One went into a man's leg, and another missed, landing on the yard somewhere, with a loud ricocheting sound. The man behind Clint fell, letting him go from the bullet wound. Another man pulled a knife from his boot. Clint was in danger. She shot again. Hannah concentrated this time, and the bullet hit his hand, knocking the knife off of his hand; instead began to bleed. The other man's leg was wet and red from blood. The one with the hand wound grabbed onto the man with the leg wound, and began to back away.

Full moon above the cold yet slightly warm yard of Fu Ji Mao shone on the shadows of two men limping away.

Hannah got close to Clint. He wasn't seriously injured. As she lifted him up, Dr. Hui and the police arrived. The police turned on the sirens and blocked off the area, and came to Hannah and Clint. The detective arrived, asking what had happened.

"What happened? I just heard gun shots. Are you okay? Are you hurt?"

"Who shot the gun at whom?"

He asked in Chinese, and although Hannah understood, she wasn't as fluent in talking. She murmured, and Dr. Hui came closer to ask,

"Are you okay, Hannah?"

"Yes, thank you. Did you see those two men?"

"No? What do you mean?"

"Well, truth is, much longer than desired, I'm afraid."

"Why did you come here? Why you didn't say anything? The police wants to know what happened here. Tell me."

"Actually, I have in my possession, a diary left by Sel Lin Chao, which is a link that I have to Summer Wu's murder, and even historical evidence toward the Nanking Massacre. Summer is Dr. Wu's daughter. I received this through Summer's will, and I wanted to see if there was any link. Of course, as she willed it, I believe this historic event must be well known. I just wanted to know more about this record."

"I heard some things from Dr. Wu, but I hadn't known the extent. Let me first tell this to the police."

"Please let them know that I am an author in America, and wanted to do some research on the Nanking Massacre. We were looking at the main sanctum in Fu Ji Mao, when we were attacked by them; I don't know who they are or why it happened to us, so please tell them as such."

"Okay, I'll do as such. Also, why don't you two come to my house today? I don't know if the hotel will be safe. I'll call them and tell them to bring your luggage out to the front. We'll check out tonight. What do you think?"

"That'd be great. Thank you, Professor Hui," replied Clint.

A few moments later, Prof. Hui explained the situation to the police, and the head policeman accepted the story; he told them to call him if they needed help, and handed Clint a business card before leaving. A few moments later, Dr. Hui called the hotel and checked out, telling them to bring the luggage to the front.

The couple and Prof. Hui rode in his car to the hotel, where they picked up the luggage, and headed to Dr. Hui's house.

As soon as they arrived at his home, Hannah opened her luggage. The documents she'd translated were gone. Thankfully, she had another copy saved on her computer. Also, it was becoming clear as to what they were seeking.

She called Sun-Soon Kim. She felt like that was the next step. Hannah stumbled over her words as she spoke in Chinese,

"Hello? May I speak to Ms. Sun-Soon Kim?"

"That's me. Who is this?"

"My name is Hannah Walter. I'm from the States and wanted to meet with you, but didn't have the time, so I'm making a call."

"Ah, Hannah, I've heard of you. Kyoo In called me and sent me mail. I was getting ready to meet with you. You're right; if you came here, you'd have to stay a few days."

"If I invite you to the States, will you come?"

"Of course. I will go if I can. I won't live long, but I'd love to reveal the truth before I do so."

"Thank you Ms. Kim. I'd love to meet with you. I just had a quick question."

"What is it?"

"When did you get to see Sel Lin Chao again?"

"It was during the purge. My husband was facing purge, and I was in danger. Someone who envied my husband called him out; he told me that morning to head to Taiwan the moment he left for work that day… from then on, I hid myself, from Beijing to Chongqing, from Chongqing to Nanjing, eventually to Taiwan. I never even saw my husband's corpse; I just took a boat to Taiwan. I looked for her, but couldn't find her until ten years afterwards. ShenLong was married by then, with a child. Kyoo In was still studying. Sister was working on helping the poor."

"Then you must have met Summer as well."

"Of course. Her name then was Nan-Hui. Nan-Hui Chung. She was such a cute and pretty child… to think she's dead…"

"Then, do you also know of her adoption to Dr. Wu?"

"Yes. A few years ago, Kyoo In sent me a letter. Told me Summer was interested in learning about her past. To tell her everything I knew. Then I remembered something sister had given me before she passed away. Nan-Hui came last year and spent a few months with me. So I told her everything and gave her the diary."

"How did sister Marta pass away?"

"Sister Marta returned from America after studying. I don't know when that was… she was much more active and healthier than I was. But then she spent most of her energy on the poor and sick. She never rested. She would spend some time organizing that diary of hers. I helped her with families, like finding families, helping with adoptions, or bringing food to the elderly. Unfortunately, cancer overtook her, and she couldn't get up afterwards. She coughed up blood. It was lung cancer. She begged me, I think she was very close to death; she asked me to give all of her diary and things to ShenLong's daughter, Summer. She asked to be buried in the Catholic church's gravesite, where her family wouldn't be able to find her. I think she meant well."

"I have one more question. You don't have to answer if you don't want to. There aren't much on you and Yul Lin in the diary. What did you do before you escaped from the Japanese military?"

Silence. Then Sun-Soon gave a deep sigh, before the words she hid deep inside finally came out, unearthed from time.

"I was brought into be used as a sex slave in the Comfort Women Unit from Korea. I was fourteen. We all were virgins, raped, then taken from place to place in their trucks. We went where they went. They did unthinkable things to us. We were alive because we couldn't die, but most of us lived in our personal hells, thinking the day our virginities were taken from us as the day we died. They then took us to Nanjing. There I met the eleven year old Yul Lin Chao."

"I see. Thank you for opening up such a difficult part of you, and for speaking for so long with me. I really want to meet you. I will definitely invite you. Please stay healthy until then."

"I guess I still have things left to do in this world, since the Lord keeps sending me people. I don't know if I can be on a plane for a long time. Thank you for spending time with me. I haven't really spoken with anyone since sister died. We've spoken for a long time. Thank you. Do be careful. I'm a bit tired…"

"Thank you, Sun-Soon. Really!"

Hannah looked around after finishing her conversation, and saw that everyone seemed to be sleeping. As soon as she hung up, Dr. Hui brought three cups of warm milk. An exhausted Clint took a cup and drank it.

Hannah also took a cup, and thought that truth was slowly being revealed, that she had to organize it and show it to the world, and that this was a duty to all those who'd survived that difficult period. Deep feelings of sadness and impression made her heart feel like it'd explode.

Twenty Nine

Dr. Hui lost his wife to cancer a few years back, and was living alone. He had a dog, which was his entire family. He got teary talking about how his wife adored the puppy, and now the puppy had grown into a dog and was his companion. Once she finished her conversation with Sun-Soon, she showed him everything she'd found at Fu Ji Mao. Dr. Hui's eyes widened in surprise, before he rushed into the study and brought a huge mirror like microscope. He looked through the microscope and said,

"This is a very important historical relic. These foot binders were used by the royalty. The picture of the dragon makes me think that it was worn by someone of royal blood. This gem which lights up in the dark… legends said that when a royalty passed away, their treasures got buried with them. I thought the last emperor Puyi's mother was buried with one… but also that scavengers stole all of them."

"Really? If it's true that the Japanese soldiers invaded China and took the treasure, oh, and also, please look at this notebook. I don't really know Chinese; I was born in America. I have no clue what it says," said Hannah, as she handed him an old notebook.

He looked at the notebook, before he buried his face into it. He kept wiping tears off of his eyes, from what seemed to be shock.

"This is truly an important historical data. It tells you exactly what the Japanese did. From locations of live experimental labs, the types of tools used, locations of Chinese, Korean, Russian, Mongolian, and Filipino comfort women locations. From Nanjing to Shanghai, Hebei, and Haerbin… it shows a lot of what they did."

"I'll take pictures of everything. Since we need to turn this into the Chinese government, I'll just take pictures. Is that all right? Oh, and what is this memo saying? It's in Chinese," said Hannah, as she handed the memo to Dr. Hui. He read it for her:

Sel Lin,

I was conflicted as I leave this to you.

But I leave this hear because it's not something I should keep, and the things I've written here are things I heard and saw; I do this to repent my status as a traitor, and so that the truth will prevent this from happening again.

The foot binder is something one of my inferiors found. I needed to take it to my superiors, but I'm going to leave it here: it's not Japan's.

I won the item in black fabric. I assume it's historical. I also leave this to you because it's not Japan's.

I give all this to you. I know you'll place it in the right hands. I know I betrayed my country and fought for my enemies, and handed many lives of the Chinese and Koreans into the hands of my enemies, but I learned my ways since meeting you, and I decided no longer to commit such crimes. I leave this as my repentance to those who suffered because of me.

Yoshihiro

Prof. Hui finished reading the memo and nodded. Hannah asked,

"Why would Yoshihiro leave all these important evidence to Sel Lin?"

"Maybe that Korean, who was a Japanese officer, was impressed by Sel Lin Chao, or maybe he loved her and wanted to do something for her, or like he said, he felt remorse and wanted to repent."

"Perhaps so," Clint answered instead.

"There's simply no way I can sleep tonight. You two can stay here as long as you'd like."

"We've done what we needed to do, so we have no more need to do so. Also, if we keep staying here, it could get dangerous for you, just like how it was for us at Fu Ji Mao. But if we invite you to America, will you be able to make it?"

"Of course. It's been a while since I saw my friend. Always. I can call the museum tomo... no, today, and see if they can bring someone related to the government. Do you want to have them come here or to the school?"

"It doesn't matter to us. But I think the school will be safer to the teacher. It could be difficult for you if the media exposes your place," Hannah suggested.

"You're right, Hannah. What do you think, Clint?"

"I feel the same way. Let's take care of it at the school in the morning," answered Clint.

As soon as Hannah finished taking the pictures, she sent it to her email account, and felt relieved for once. A few moments later, she slept for a few hours in Dr. Hui's guestroom, woke up, and headed to Jin Ling University.

As soon as they arrived, Dr. Hui must have already told the university head, as he came out to meet them. Head of the National museum, various news channels and media representatives were all in attendance, looking for a better location.

The head of the museum performed a special event where he took back the foot binder, the bead, and notebook in front of the Jin Ling University students at the main hall of the school gym, and people from the central government also attended the event. The head of the museum stated the possibility of the foot binder and the bead belonging to Puyi's mother, and the notebook as a key evidence in proving various war crimes by Japan, including their continued ignorance toward the issue of comfort women.The government officials thanked Hannah and Clint and completed the ceremony.

Once Hannah and Clint completed their schedule, they found their heart light, knowing that they knew everything, yet found another weight on them. They bid Dr. Hui a good bye before getting on a plane headed for the States.

Hannah was able to spend the time organizing and was able to realize what she really loved and what she had to do. Her relationship with Clint was stronger. She was no longer a weakening woman in her late fifties; she found a way to live out the rest of her life, She'd busily fill her time organizing and to fill that time with new things; such time was waiting for her. Hannah carefully gripped the hand of sleeping Clint. Clint tried to hug Hannah, but the place was a business seat on an airplane, not the hotel or their home. Not yet…

Once Hannah returned home to the States, she began to button up the story from the beginning to the end, one by one. Summer's death and the life of Sel Lin Chao, and the countless number of death…, she believed that such death should not be wasted on inaccurate history. That's what Hannah had to do.

She contacted Sun-Soon. She left Taiwan, spent a few days with Dr. Wu trying to get used to time and the long travel, and would come to Washington, D.C. with Dr. Wu.

To celebrate the publication of the novel, *Tears of the Yangtze*, Sun-Soon Kim from Taiwan, Dr. Hui from China, the Wu couple from California, and their daughter Naomi from Washington all planned to attend the event. Hannah and Clint called and organized a way for the comfort women in Korea to join them, as most of the women forced to serve as Comfort women under the Japanese military were from Korea.

At the Hilton hotel in front of the White House in Washington, D.C., many local Asians attended the event, and many Asian leaders and media members came to publicize the publishing event of her book. Dr. Wu then introduced Sun-Soon Kim.

"Ms. Sun-Soon Kim experienced the horrors of comfort women sex slavery in Nanjing. She's a Korean comfort woman, who dedicated her life to others and worked hard for the independence of her own country. She survived difficulties through one of the most difficult period in our history,"

Sun-Soon began to speak,

"I was a comfort woman. Sometimes, I was raped by thirty to forty Japanese soldiers in a day. They didn't treat me like a human being. I thought that even if I died, I didn't want to die as a comfort woman, so my friends and I tried to escape, but I was the only one that survived. I now understand why I had to stay alive. It was for truth."

Her hands and voice shook, and she couldn't say anything else, but everyone understood what she'd said.

Dr. Wu then explained the life of Sel Lin Chao, who was a real person, through his life story as Kyoo In.

They then drove over to a Memorial. The memorial platform said, "Voice of Truth," and three other Korean comfort women ladies sat beneath it. There was a big screen hanging next to them. Many people had attended the event and sat across from the screen. As soon as it began, the data that Hannah had found were translated and projected, and the media members who gathered there missed not a single thing.

Of all of the things that Japan had denied regarding the Nanking Massacre, the corpses on the riverbed; bloody Yangtze River water, naked and violated women, headless corpses, a fetus seen through split stomach of a dead woman… all of these things that Japanese government wanted to bury were on the screen. The tools used for live experiments, plan information on comfort women distribution, foot binder and bead that the soldiers had stolen, picture of a Japanese soldier and Sel Lin Chao, and lastly, the apology of Yoshihiro, a Korean serving as a Japanese soldier projected onto the screen, one by one. People began to yell, their hands in a tight fist.

"Apologize and repent, Abe! Truthfully! To the world! To the victims! Apologize to the 300,000 Chinese souls! Apologize to the 200,000 Comfort women of the world! Apologize! Apologize! Repent! Repent! Indemnify! Indemnify! Apologize!" They yelled in one voice.

A flock of seagulls flew and circled around the platform where the three ladies from Korea, Sun-Soon Kim in a nice hanbok gifted by Hannah, Summer's sister Naomi, wife of Dr. Wu and Dr. Wu, Prof. Hui, and Hannah and Clint were sitting, then sat on the reflecting pool.

When the event was about to end, the seagulls powerfully flew up to the West, in a v formation.

Author's Note

A few years ago, I came across a documentary on the Nanjing Massacre, which was a hugely criminal act; I couldn't calm the anger in me. Even though the picture passed by in a glance: the trashed corpses with eyes still open and their arms wide open toward the sky, surprised faces of the corpses, not expecting the end of their lives, wooden stakes on women's lower parts, the split stomachs of women and the dead fetus inside; the horrible criminal acts of the Japanese Empire; I could see their last words, "Have mercy!" which they probably couldn't have even uttered in their last moments. They were in my head and refused to leave, making it difficult for me to sleep.

I had to do something. I wanted to be their voice in this world, slowly forgetting those who died without a right to a voice as time flowed by, and needed to dig out the fading events of history and consciousness, so that humans never deal with such atrocity again.

This was when I learned about the death of Irish Chang, who was a journalist with AP and Chicago Tribune.

After receiving details on the details of her alleged suicide, and her information on "Rape of Nanjing," I decided that I wanted to help close the eyes of those who couldn't say what they wanted to say in the face of death.

This novel was written with the intent for Japan to properly apologize and pay reparations for its crimes against China, Korea, Vietnam, Philippines, and other Asian countries, as well as their actions of massacre on those living in Shanghai and Nanjing all for the purpose of imperialism and wealth, and to provide a way to move forward into the future, properly; I sometimes acted through my own eyes, or from a third party individual, as we climbed back into history to speak with the mouths of the dead.

Recently, Prime Minister Shinzo Abe has refused to mention their wrongdoings regarding comfort women issue, to apologize, or to provide reparations for them. World expects him to lead his country in apologizing for their wrongdoings. But he merely said, "I don't want to burden the future generation with the burdens of the past," without taking any action to lessen such burden, disappointing nations and media once more.

This novel is centered on a historical event, and the characters are fictional and any similar or same names of characters are purely coincidental.

As I wrote this novel, I referenced evidence where Japan as the perpetrator justified their action by stating as a "necessary behavior for good," and history as seen through the eyes of the Chinese, who could see where the Japanese failed to shrink, bury, or alter the evidence.

References

Hu, Hualing. *American Goddess at the Rape of Nanking: The Courage of Minnie Vautrin*. Carbondale: Southern Illinois UP, 2000. Print.

바베르크. "발발 77 주년을 맞은 중일전쟁을 다시 생각하며." *허핑턴포스트*. Web. 08 Apr. 2016.
<http://www.huffingtonpost.kr/bawerk/story_b_5562746.html>.

"북한군사훈련 팔로군에서 시행." *네이버 뉴스 라이브러리*. 동아일보. Web. 08 Apr. 2016.
<http://newslibrary.naver.com/viewer/index.nhn?rticleId=1948111900209201021
>.

"China-Japan Friction Saves 'Comfort Women' Houses in Nanjing." - *All China Women's Federation*. Web. 08 Apr. 2016.
<http://www.womenofchina.cn/womenofchina/html1/news/china/17/4517-1.htm>.

Benson, Heidi. "Historian Iris Chang Won Many Battles / The War She Lost Raged within." *SFGate*. 17 Apr. 2005. Web. 09 Apr. 2016.
<http://www.sfgate.com/health/article/Historian-Iris-Chang-won-many-battles-The-war-2679354.php>.

"Death Toll of the Nanking Massacre." *Wikipedia*. Wikimedia Foundation. Web. 09 Apr. 2016.

"Nanking Massacre Denial." *Wikipedia*. Wikimedia Foundation. Web. 09 Apr. 2016.

"Contest to Kill 100 People Using a Sword." *Wikipedia*. Wikimedia Foundation. Web. 09 Apr. 2016.

"International Military Tribunal for the Far East." *Wikipedia*. Wikimedia Foundation. Web. 09 Apr. 2016.

"Nanjing War Crimes Tribunal." *Wikipedia*. Wikimedia Foundation. Web. 09 Apr. 2016.

"Battle of Nanking." *Wikipedia*. Wikimedia Foundation. Web. 09 Apr. 2016.

"City of Life and Death." *Wikipedia*. Wikimedia Foundation. Web. 09 Apr. 2016.

"The Flowers of War." *Wikipedia*. Wikimedia Foundation. Web. 09 Apr. 2016.

"Nanking (2007 Film)." *Wikipedia*. Wikimedia Foundation. Web. 09 Apr. 2016.

"The Truth about Nanjing." *Wikipedia*. Wikimedia Foundation. Web. 09 Apr. 2016.